作家榜®经典名著

读经典名著，认准作家榜

GITANJALI

吉檀迦利

[印]泰戈尔——著

西 蒙——译

本书译自

印度新德里 UBSPD 出版社 2003 年英文版《吉檀迦利》，英文版为泰戈尔从多部孟加拉文诗集选译诗歌集结而成。

致威廉·罗森斯坦*

---

* 威廉·罗森斯坦(1872—1945),英国画家、绘图员、大学教授和艺术作家。一生致力于艺术创作,其肖像画作品广受欢迎。

朗兰湾的早晨 ［法］阿尔弗雷德·西斯莱

When I leave from hence let this be my parting word that what I have seen is unsurpassable. I have tasted of the hidden honey of this lotus yonder that expands on the ocean of light and thus am I blessed, let this be my parting word. In this playhouse of infinite forms I have had my play and here have I caught sight of him that eludes all forms. All my living body and limbs have thrilled with his touch who is beyond touch — and if the end comes here let it come — Let this be my parting word.

《吉檀迦利》手稿

目录

叶芝序
人类所有的渴望,
都在他的诗歌里　　　　　　　　　　01

吉檀迦利
第一部分　1—35 首　　　　　　　　001
第二部分　36—56 首　　　　　　　071
第三部分　57—85 首　　　　　　　139
第四部分　86—103 首　　　　　　　213

附录
1913 年诺贝尔文学奖颁奖典礼致辞　　262
泰戈尔诺贝尔文学奖获奖致辞　　　　272
泰戈尔生平年表　　　　　　　　　　282

叶芝序[1]

人类所有的渴望，
　　　都在他的诗歌里

I

几天前，我和一位杰出的孟加拉医学博士说起："我不懂德文，但要是有哪位德国诗人的翻译作品感动了我，我就会去大英博物馆，找到英语书籍，这可以让我了解他生平的一些事情，以及他的思想历史。拉宾德拉纳特·泰戈尔的散文翻译让我热血沸腾，我很多年都没读到这样的作品了。但要不是某个印度旅行者讲给我，我对泰戈尔的生平，和他写这些作品时的思想轨迹，都一无所知。"

---

[1] 此文为威廉·巴特勒·叶芝于1912年为初版《吉檀迦利》写就的序，标题为译者所加。威廉·巴特勒·叶芝（1865—1939），爱尔兰诗人、剧作家，1923年获诺贝尔文学奖。被诗人T. S. 艾略特誉为"当代最伟大的诗人"。一生创作丰富，备受敬仰。

在他看来，我被感动是很自然的事，因为他说："我每天都读拉宾德拉纳特，只消读上一行，就会忘记这世上所有的烦恼。"

我说："对于一位活在理查二世统治时期的英国人来说，要是他读到彼得拉克或是但丁作品的翻译，肯定找不到什么书籍来解答他的疑问，而只能去请教某位佛罗伦萨的银行家，或是伦巴第的商人，就像我向您请教一样。据我所知，新的文艺复兴已在你们国内开始了，诗歌如此丰富而又简练，而我却只是听到些传闻而已。"

他回答道："我们还有其他诗人，但无人能与他比肩。我们称之为拉宾德拉纳特的时代。在我看来，欧洲没有哪位诗人在欧洲能像他在我们中间那样著名。他在音乐领域也如在诗歌领域那样伟大，从印度西部一直到缅甸，只要是讲孟加拉语的地方，他的歌曲都会被传唱。他十九岁就出名了，那时他写出了第一本小说，而他稍后几年写的戏剧，至今还在加尔各答上演。我非常崇拜他生命的圆满。他在很年轻的时候，描写了大量的自然景致，会一整天都坐在花园里。大概在二十五岁到三十五岁期间，他承受了巨大的痛苦，写出了我们语言里最美的情诗。"

接着,他极为动情地说道:"我十七岁那年,从他的情诗中所得到的,永远无法用语言表述出来。打那以后,他的艺术变得更为深沉,开始加入宗教和哲学的思想,人类所有的灵感都出现在他的赞歌里。在我们所有的圣人中,他是第一位不拒绝生活的人,反而大声赞美生命,所以我们对他如此爱戴。"我也许没完全记住他精心选择的词语,但对他的想法却记得真真切切。"不久前,他在我们的一处教堂——我们梵社的人借用你们的英文词'教堂'——做礼拜读诗,那是加尔各答最大的教堂,里面挤满了人,人们甚至站到窗台上,连大街上都人满为患,无法通行。"

其他印度人来看我,他们对这个人的尊敬,在我们的世界里听起来很奇特,在我们这里,无论大事还是小情,我们都会隐藏在同一面纱下,表面上很诙谐,又半含轻蔑。我们在建造大教堂时,对我们的伟人是否有同样的敬仰?"每天凌晨三点——我知道的,因为我见过,"一个人对我说道,"他一动不动地坐着,冥想神灵。他的父亲是一位宗教导师,他有时会一直坐到隔日;有一回在河上,他面对美丽的风景沉浸于冥想,桨手们足足等了八个小时,才继续前行。"

他接着给我讲述了泰戈尔先生的家族,从这个摇篮中走出过好几代伟大的人物。

"如今,"他说,"就有艺术家高戈南德拉纳特·泰戈尔和阿巴宁德拉纳特·泰戈尔;还有德威仁德拉纳特,拉宾德拉纳特的哥哥,他是一位伟大的哲学家。松鼠们沿着树枝爬过来,爬到他的膝上,鸟儿们飞落在他的手上。"

我留意到,在这些人的想法当中,有一种可见的美感和意义,如同尼采的信条,即我们不要去相信那些道德或文化之美,如果它们不能或迟或早地在真实的事物上留下印记。

我说:"在东方,你们知道如何让一个家族保持辉煌。有一天,有位博物馆的馆长指给我看一个皮肤黝黑的小个子男人,他正在布置馆里的中国画。馆长说:'他是日本天皇的世袭鉴赏师,居于此位的家族第十四代传人。'"

他回答道:"当拉宾德拉纳特还是个孩童,家里环绕着他的就是文学和音乐。"

我想到那些诗歌的丰富与简练,于是说:"在你们国家,有很多宣传性的文章和评论性的文章吗?

我们要作太多这样的文章,尤其是我自己的国家,以至于我们的心灵逐渐变得不再有创造性,而我们对此无能为力。如果我们的生命不是一场持续的斗争,我们就不会具有品味,不知道什么是好的,找不到听众和读者。我们五分之四的精力都花费在与低劣品味的争斗之中,在我们自己的思想里,或是在他人的思想里。"

"我理解,"他答道,"我们也有我们的宣传性文章。在村子里,他们朗诵改编自中世纪梵文的神话长诗,经常会加入一些段落,告诫人们一定要尽职尽责。"

II

数天来,我一直把翻译手稿带在身边,在火车上、公共汽车上,或是餐馆里阅读,而且我经常不得不合上它,以免陌生人看到它多么令我感动。这些抒情诗——我的印度朋友告诉我,在原文中充满微妙的节奏、无法翻译的精致色泽、创新的韵律——它们的思想展示出一个世界，我一生都梦寐以求的世界。至高文化的杰作，却自然如草木生长。

诗歌与宗教合二为一的传统世代相传，它取自已知和未知的隐喻和情感，又将学者和贵族的思想带回给芸芸众生。如果孟加拉文明保持完整，如果共同的心灵——作为神圣的一体——一直存续，就不会像我们一样，破碎成为一打彼此毫无知觉的心灵，那么，甚至这些诗歌中最为微妙的部分，用不了几代人，也会流传到路边的乞丐那儿。在英格兰只有一个伟大心灵的年代，乔叟写出了《特洛伊罗斯与克瑞西达》，虽然他写作是为了被阅读，或是被诵读——因为我们的时代飞快地到来了——但他还是被游吟诗人歌唱了一阵子。

和乔叟的先行者一样，拉宾德拉纳特为词配曲。他明白每时每刻自己都极为丰富，极为自发，感情充沛，充满惊喜，因为他的所作所为，没有丝毫奇怪或不自然，不需要任何辩解。这些诗句不会躺在印刷精美的小册子里，置于淑女桌上，她们用慵懒的手翻开书页，或许在为毫无意义的生活叹息，而她们也仅只了解这样的生活；这些诗句也不会被大学生们携带，当生活开始后便被搁置一边；但是随着世代更迭，旅行者们会在高速公路上哼唱它们,桨手们会在河上哼唱它们。而情人们在彼此等待时,会低声诵读这些诗句,会发现这份上帝之爱的神奇海湾,然后将他们自己更为痛苦的热情沐浴其中,并获得新生。每时每刻,诗人之心都谦逊而完整地流往他们,因为这颗心知道他们会理解,并以他们的生活环境充盈自己。

旅行者穿着红褐色的衣裳,身上不落尘土;少女在床上摸索王室情人花冠上掉落的花瓣;仆人或新娘守候在空房子里,等待主人归来;这些都是转向上帝之心的意象。鲜花与河流,海螺的鸣响,印度历七月的大雨,炎热的炙烤,是相逢或分离时心境的意象;一个男人泛舟于河上,弹着琵琶,仿佛中国画充满神秘感的人物之一,就是上帝自身。对于我们来说无比陌生的整个民族和整个文明,似乎都被带入了这份想象;我们没被感动,不是由于陌生,而是我们已遇见自己的意象,仿佛我们已在罗塞蒂的杨柳林里穿行,或者第一次在文学里听到我们的声音,恍若在梦中。

自从文艺复兴以来,欧洲圣人的写作——不管他们的隐喻以及思想的整体结构对我们来说多么熟悉——已不再吸引我们的注意力。我们知道最终必须放弃这个世界,我们习惯在疲惫或欣喜的瞬间考虑主动放弃；但我们已阅读过如此多的诗歌，欣赏过如此多的绘画，倾听过如此多的音乐，肉体的哭喊和灵魂的哭喊似乎合为一体，又怎能残忍粗暴地放弃？圣伯纳德[1]覆盖住双眼，不让它们流连于瑞士湖水的美景，或是《启示录》中激烈的言辞，我们与其有何共同之处呢？如果愿意，我们也许可以在这本书中找到谦逊之辞。

"我已获准离去。和我说再见吧，我的兄弟们！我向你们所有人鞠躬，转身离去。我把家门钥匙交还——放弃了对房子的拥有。我只祈求你们最后的善语。我们常年为邻，我得到的，多于我能够给予的。而现在天已破晓，照亮我黑暗角落的灯也已熄灭。召唤已来，我准备好启程了。"远自肯皮斯[2]和圣十字若望[3]的时候，这就已经是我们自己心境的哭喊："因为我热爱生命，我知道我也将热爱死亡。"

这本书洞察了一切，不仅仅是我们想要离去的想法。我们并不知道自己热爱上帝，也几乎没信过他；

---

1 圣伯纳德（1090—1153），法国教士、罗马教皇顾问。
2 肯皮斯(1380—1471)，中世纪晚期的天主教神职人员，其《论模仿基督》一书是最著名的基督教著作之一。
3 圣十字若望（1542—1591），西班牙天主教牧师、神秘学家，是西班牙反宗教改革的重要人物。

然而回顾我们的生命,在林间探路时,在山冈孤寂之处的喜悦中,在我们所做的神秘断言里,徒劳地,在我们所爱的女人身上,我们发现了这种创造隐秘甜蜜的情感。"你竟如芸芸众生的一员,不知不觉进入我心,在我生命转眼即逝的瞬间,盖上了永恒的印鉴。"这已不再是牢狱与苦难的神圣,而是一种升华,恍如进到画家更强烈的情绪中,画出尘埃与阳光。我们在圣方济各[1]和威廉·布莱克[2]那里寻找相仿的声音,即使他们在我们暴烈的历史中显得如此不同。

III

我们撰写长文,或许其中并没有哪页有让写作成为一种乐趣的质量,或者在整体设计上自信满满,正如我们争斗赚钱,让头脑里充满政治——所为皆是无聊之事——而泰戈尔先生,如同印度文明自身,满足于探索心灵,把自己交给自发性。他似乎经常将自己

---

[1] 圣方济各(1182—1226),天主教方济各会和方济各女修会的创始人。
[2] 威廉·布莱克(1757—1827),英国浪漫主义诗人。

的生命与那些比我们的时尚活得更久的人相比,与世上看起来更有分量的人相比,并且总是保持谦卑,似乎他只确认,他的路对于他是最好的。"回家的人们瞥见我,露出笑意,让我羞愧不已。我像个女乞丐般坐着,用裙子蒙住我的脸。当他们问我想要何物时,我垂眼不答。"而在另一时刻,想起他的生命曾有过另一种形态,他会说:"在正直与邪恶的争斗中,我荒废了无数时光,现在,我那空虚日子的玩伴的快乐,把我的心拉向他;而我并不明白,为何会忽然召唤我,去面对那无用的冲突。"

一种人们在别处文学中所找不到的天真与朴素,让鸟儿和草叶靠近他,如同靠近孩童,让季节的变换成为重大的事件,先于我们那些产生在它们和我们之间的想法。有时,我会好奇,不知他得之于孟加拉文学,还是宗教;有时,我还会记起,鸟儿落在他哥哥的手上,我愉快地想到这是遗传的,一种世代生长的神秘,就像特里斯坦人或皮拉诺人的礼仪。

的确,当他说起孩童,他用了如此多的篇幅,如此用心,让人不敢肯定他是否也在说圣人:"他们堆起沙堡,玩耍空贝壳。用枯叶编成小船,笑呵呵地推送到广阔的深海。孩子们在世界的海滨玩耍。他们不会游泳,不懂撒网。渔夫潜海找寻珍珠,商人们乘船远航,孩子们拾起卵石又随手扔掉。他们不去寻宝,他们不知如何撒网。"

1912年9月

海景 [巴西] 坎迪多·波尔蒂纳里

"莲花盛开的那天，唉，我不自觉地走神了。"

On the day when the lotus bloomed, alas, my mind was straying, and I knew it not.

吉檀迦利

第一部分／1—35首

1

你让我永生,这是你的快乐。你不停地清空这脆弱的容器,又不停地用新鲜生命将其充盈。

你翻山越岭带在身边的小小苇笛,用它吹出永新的曲调。

你不朽的双手,触摸我小小的心儿,让它快乐四溢,难以言喻。

你把无数的礼物,交到我小小的手上。时光流逝,你一直在倾注,而这容器从未被注满。

Thou hast made me endless, such is thy pleasure. This frail vessel thou emptiest again and again, and fillest it ever with fresh life.

This little flute of a reed thou hast carried over hills and dales, and hast breathed through it melodies eternally new.

At the immortal touch of thy hands my little heart loses its limits in joy and gives birth to utterance ineffable.

Thy infinite gifts come to me only on these very small hands of mine. Ages pass, and still thou pourest, and still there is room to fill.

2

当你命令我歌唱时,我的心骄傲得几乎要裂开。望着你的脸,我的眼中盈满泪水。

我生命中粗糙刺耳的杂声融为甜美的谐音,我对你的崇拜像一只快乐的鸟,展翅飞越大海。

我知道你喜欢我的歌唱。我知道只有作为一名歌手,我才会来到你的面前。

我用歌声舒展的翼尖,触碰你的双脚,在过去我从未奢望过。

沉醉于歌唱的喜悦,我迷失了自己,称你为朋友,而你却是我的主人。

When thou commandest me to sing it seems that my heart would break with pride; and I look to thy face, and tears come to my eyes.

All that is harsh and dissonant in my life melts into one sweet harmony—and my adoration spreads wings like a glad bird on its flight across the sea.

I know thou takest pleasure in my singing. I know that only as a singer I come before thy presence.

I touch by the edge of the far-spreading wing of my song thy feet which I could never aspire to reach.

Drunk with the joy of singing I forget myself and call thee friend who art my lord.

3

我不知你是如何歌唱的,我的主人!我只能安静而惊讶地倾听。

你的音乐之光照亮了这个世界。你的音乐气息弥漫天际。你的音乐圣泉冲开所有的石障,奔流不息。

我的心渴望加入你的歌唱,却发不出声响。我想张口,但呢喃之语不成曲调,我只能困惑地呼喊。啊,你用无尽的音乐之网,俘获了我的心,我的主人!

I know not how thou singest, my master! I ever listen in silent amazement.

The light of thy music illumines the world. The life breath of thy music runs from sky to sky. The holy stream of thy music breaks through all stony obstacles and rushes on.

My heart longs to join in thy song, but vainly struggles for a voice. I would speak, but speech breaks not into song, and I cry out baffled. Ah, thou hast made my heart captive in the endless meshes of thy music, my master!

4

我生命的生命,我永远要保持身体的洁净,因为我知道,你生生不息的抚慰,会落在我的肢体上。

我要摒弃思想中所有的谎言,因为我知道,你就是那真理,照亮我心灵的智性之光。

我要驱除心中所有的恶魔,让我的爱留在花中;因为我知道,你的座椅,就安放在我内心最隐秘的圣殿。

我要努力在行动中展示你,因为我知道,是你赐予我力量前行。

Life of my life, I shall ever try to keep my body pure, knowing that thy living touch is upon all my limbs.

I shall ever try to keep all untruths out from my thoughts, knowing that thou art that truth which has kindled the light of reason in my mind.

I shall ever try to drive all evils away from my heart and keep my love in flower, knowing that thou hast thy seat in the inmost shrine of my heart.

And it shall be my endeavour to reveal thee in my actions, knowing it is thy power gives me strength to act.

5

我请求懈怠一会儿,坐在你身边。手头的工作以后再完成。

见不到你,我的心不知止歇,工作就会变成无边苦海中的苦役。

今日,夏天已来到我的窗前,轻叹低语;而蜜蜂在繁花盛开的园林里飞来飞去。

现在,是时候和你面对面悄悄坐着,在静谧闲暇中吟唱生命的献歌。

I ask for a moment's indulgence to sit by thy side. The works that I have in hand I will finish afterwards.

Away from the sight of thy face my heart knows no rest nor respite, and my work becomes an endless toil in a shoreless sea of toil.

Today the summer has come at my window with its sighs and murmurs; and the bees are plying their minstrelsy at the court of the flowering grove.

Now it is time to sit quite, face to face with thee, and to sing dedication of life in this silent and overflowing leisure.

6

摘下这朵花，拿去吧，别犹豫！别让它凋谢，坠入尘埃。

它也许在你的花环上找不到位置，但请你将它摘下，用采摘的痛楚来使它荣耀。我担心在我觉醒之前，日光将尽，错过奉献的时刻。

虽然它的颜色不够浓郁，花香清淡，请你仍用这朵花侍奉，趁着还有时间，将它摘下。

Pluck this little flower and take it, delay not! I fear lest it droop and drop into the dust.

It may not find a place in thy garland, but honour it with a touch of pain from thy hand and pluck it. I fear lest the day end before I am aware, and the time of offering go by.

Though its colour be not deep and its smell be faint, use this flower in thy service and pluck it while there is time.

在圣马梅的爱恋 [法] 阿尔弗雷德·西斯莱

7

我的歌卸下她的饰物。她没有了衣饰的骄奢。饰物只会玷污我们的结合；它们会挡在你我之间；叮叮当当地淹没你的低语。

在你面前，我作为诗人的虚荣羞愧地消隐。哦，诗歌的主人，我盘坐于你的脚下。请让我的生命变得简单直接，如同一支苇笛，盈满你的音乐。

My song has put off her adornments. She has no pride of dress and decoration. Ornaments would mar our union; they would come between thee and me; their jingling would drown thy whispers.

My poet's vanity dies in shame before thy sight. O master poet, I have sat down at thy feet. Only let me make my life simple and straight, like a flute of reed for thee to fill with music.

小巷 [法] 皮尔·波纳尔

8

那个孩子身着王袍,脖子上挂满珠宝,失去了游戏中的所有快乐;他的衣物让他步履蹒跚。

担心服饰会被磨损,或是染上尘土,他与世隔离,甚至不敢动弹。

母亲,华丽的束缚让孩子止步于健康的尘世,剥夺了参与芸芸众生盛大集会的权利,这毫无益处。

The child who is decked with prince's robes and who has jewelled chains round his neck loses all pleasure in his play; his dress hampers him at every step.

In fear that it may be frayed, or stained with dust he keeps himself from the world, and is afraid even to move.

Mother, it is no gain, thy bondage of finery, if it keep one shut off from the healthful dust of the earth, if it rob one of the right of entrance to the great fair of common human life.

9

噢，痴人，想把自己背在自己的肩上！
噢，乞丐，竟然来到自家门口乞讨！

请把你所有的负担交到他的手上，他能承担一切，绝不要悔恨回顾。

你的欲望的气息，会立即吹熄它接触到的灯火。欲望不圣洁——别从它不洁的手中接过礼物。只接受神圣之爱的给予。

O Fool, try to carry thyself upon thy own shoulders! O beggar, to come beg at thy own door!

Leave all thy burdens on his hands who can bear all, and never look behind in regret.

Thy desire at once puts out the light from the lamp it touches with its breath. It is unholy — take not thy gifts through its unclean hands. Accept only what is offered by sacred love.

10

这是你的脚凳,你的双足只在最贫穷低贱而无家可归的人群中歇息。

当我试图向你鞠躬时,我的敬意无法抵达你双足歇息的深处,它们只在最贫穷低贱而无家可归的人群中歇息。

你衣衫褴褛,行走在最贫穷低贱而无家可归的人群中,傲慢永远无法抵达那里。

在最贫穷低贱而迷失的人群中,你与无伴的人为伍,我的心从未找到那里。

Here is thy footstool and there rest thy feet where live the poorest, and lowliest, and lost.

When I try to bow to thee, my obeisance cannot reach down to the depth where thy feet rest among the poorest, and lowliest, and lost.

Pride can never approach to where thou walkest in the clothes of the humble among the poorest, and lowliest, and lost.

My heart can never find its way to where thou keepest company with the companionless among the poorest, the lowliest, and the lost.

11

别再手数珠串诵经念咒了！在四门紧闭的寺庙里，在孤寂幽暗的角落，你在礼拜谁？睁开眼睛，神并不在你的面前！

他与锄着干硬土地的农夫在一起，与碎石铺路的工人在一起。无论晴天还是下雨，他与他们在一起，衣服上满是尘土。脱下你的圣袍吧，像他一样，脚踏蒙尘的实地吧！

救赎？哪里能寻到救赎？我们的主人，他自己愉悦地戴上创造的锁链；和我们所有的人永远连系在一起。

别再冥思苦想了，抛开你那些花朵和熏香！即使你的衣服破损弄脏了，又有何妨？去找他吧，眉间挂着汗水，和他一起辛苦劳作。

Leave this chanting and singing and telling of beads! Whom dost thou worship in this lonely dark corner of a temple with doors all shut? Open thine eyes and see thy God is not before thee!

He is there where the tiller is tilling the hard ground and where the pathmaker is breaking stones. He is with them in sun and in shower, and his garment is covered with dust. Put of thy holy mantle and even like him come down on the dusty soil!

Deliverance? Where is this deliverance to be found? Our master himself has joyfully taken upon him the bonds of creation; he is bound with us all for ever.

Come out of thy meditations and leave aside thy flowers and incense! What harm is there if thy clothes become tattered and stained? Meet him and stand by him in toil and in sweat of thy brow.

城市边缘的棚户区 ［巴西］坎迪多·波尔蒂纳里

12

我的旅途漫长而遥远。

我乘着黎明第一缕光明之车出发,穿越荒凉的世界,车辙遍布星球。

这是最遥远的旅程,让你最接近自己;这是最复杂的训练,引你听到至简的曲调。

旅人要敲开每一道陌生的门,才能找到自己的家。一个人要漫游遍外面的世界,才能最终抵达内心最深处的圣殿。

我四处张望,然后才合上双眼说:"原来你在这儿!"

"噢,在哪里啊?"如此的疑问与呼喊,融入千溪泪水,而一句承诺,"我在!"漫过了整个世界。

The time that my journey takes is long and the way of it long.

I came out on the chariot of the first gleam of light, and pursued my voyage through the wildernesses of worlds leaving my track on many a star and planet.

It is the most distant course that comes nearest to thyself, and that training is the most intricate which leads to the utter simplicity of a tune.

The traveller has to knock at every alien door to come to his own, and one has to wander through all the outer worlds to reach the innermost shrine at the end.

My eyes strayed far and wide before I shut them and said "Here art thou!"

The question and the cry "Oh, where?" melt into tears of a thousand streams and deluge the world with the flood of the assurance "I am!"

13

我想唱的歌,至今尚未唱出。

我花费掉整日时光,一直在调试乐器。

那一时刻尚未到来,歌词尚未写好;我心里满是希冀的烦恼。

花朵尚未打开,身边的风儿叹息而过。

我尚未见过他的面容,尚未听到他的声音;只听过他温柔的步履,从我屋前路过。

整整一天,我为他在地上摆好座椅;而灯尚未点亮,我无法请他走进我的家门。

我期待着与他见面,而会面的时间尚未到来。

The song that I came to sing remains unsung to this day.

I have spent my days in stringing and in unstringing my instrument.

The time has not come true, the words have not been rightly set; only there is the agony of wishing in my heart.

The blossom has not opened; only the wind is sighing by.

I have not seen his face, nor have I listened to his voice; only I have heard his gentle footsteps from the road before my house.

The livelong day has passed in spreading his seat on the floor; but the lamp has not been lit and I cannot ask him into my house.

I live in the hope of meeting with him; but this meeting is not yet.

我想唱的歌，
至今尚未唱出。

14

我的欲望很多,我的哭泣可怜,而你总是通过强硬的拒绝拯救我;如今,这份坚定的仁慈,已紧密地交织在我的生命里。

日复一日,你让我配得上那简单而伟大的礼物,你给予我,而我不曾索求——天空和光明,身体、生命和心灵——拯救我于过度欲望的危境。

有时我倦怠地无所事事,有时我醒来急匆匆寻求目标;你都残忍地隐身,不让我见到你。

日复一日,你不停地拒绝我,拯救我于软弱不定的欲望的险境,以使我值得你满心接纳。

My desires are many and my cry is pitiful, but ever didst thou save me by hard refusals; and this strong mercy has been wrought into my life through and through.

Day by day thou art making me worthy of the simple, great gifts that thou gavest to me unasked — this sky and the light, this body and the life and the mind — saving me from perils of overmuch desire.

There are times when I languidly linger and times when I awaken and hurry in search of my goal; but cruelly thou hidest thyself from before me.

Day by day thou art making me worthy of thy full acceptance by refusing me ever and anon, saving me from perils of weak, uncertain desire.

15

我来为你歌唱。在你的大厅里,我在角落有个位置。

在你的世界里,我无事可做,我无用的生命只能弹出毫无意义的曲调。

午夜暗黑的寺庙,当钟声响起,默祷的时刻到来,命令我吧,我的主人,上前为你歌唱。

清晨,金色的竖琴已调好,召见我吧。

I am here to sing thee songs. In this hall of thine I have a corner seat.

In thy world I have no work to do; my useless life can only break out in tunes without a purpose.

When the hour strikes for thy silent worship at the dark temple of midnight, command me, my master, to stand before thee to sing.

When in the morning air the golden harp is tuned, honour me, commanding my presence.

16

我收到了这世界节日的请柬,生命受到祝福。我的双眼已见,我的双耳已闻。

我要在节日演奏我的乐器,我已尽力而为。

而现在,我要问,时辰是否终于到来,我是否可以进去见到你,为你献上我静默的问候?

I have had my invitation to this world's festival, and thus my life has been blessed. My eyes have seen and my ears have heard.

It was my part at this feast to play upon my instrument, and I have done all I could.

Now, I ask, has the time come at last when I may go in and see thy face and offer thee my silent salutation?

春天的声音 〔美〕乔治·J·斯坦格尔

17

我只在安静地等候爱,把自己最终交到他的手上。这便是为何如此迟缓,为何我对这样的延误深感内疚。

他们带着法典而来,要牢牢地约束我;而我总是躲开他们,因我一直在等候爱,把自己最终交到他的手上。

人们总是责怪我漫不经心,我也知道他们的指责是对的。

集市已散,忙碌的人们都干完了活儿。那些来喊我的人们,恼怒地无功而返。我只在等候爱,以把自己最终交到他的手上。

I am only waiting for love to give myself up at last into his hands. That is why it is so late and why I have been guilty of such omissions.

They come with their laws and their codes to bind me fast; but I evade them ever, for I am only waiting for love to give myself up at last into his hands.

People blame me and call me heedless; I doubt not they are right in their blame.

The market day is over and work is all done for the busy. Those who came to call me in vain have gone back in anger. I am only waiting for love to give myself up at last into his hands.

18

雾霭沉沉,天色向晚。啊,爱呀,为何你让我在门外独自等候?

正午忙碌时分,我身处人群之中,但在这黑暗孤寂的日子里,我只期盼见到你。

要是你不见我,把我彻底抛在一边,我真不知如何才能度过这漫长的雨天。

我凝视着遥远阴郁的天空,我的心和不宁的风儿一同彷徨哭泣。

Clouds heap upon clouds and it darkens. Ah, love, why dost thou let me wait outside at the door all alone?

In the busy moments of the noontide work I am with the crowd, but on this dark lonely day it is only for thee that I hope.

If thou showest me not thy face, if thou leavest me wholly aside, I know not how I am to pass these long, rainy hours.

I keep gazing on the far-away gloom of the sky, and my heart wanders wailing with the restless wind.

19

你要是不说话,我就以你的静默盈满我心,隐忍承受。我要沉静守候,如同群星守护的夜晚,耐心地低着头。

清晨一定会到来,黑暗会隐退,你的声音会如金泉,冲破天际倾泻而下。

那时你的话语,将在我的每一个鸟巢振翅歌唱,而你的旋律,将盛开在我所有林园的花朵中。

If thou speakest not I will fill my heart with thy silence and endure it. I will keep still and wait like the night with starry vigil and its head bent low with patience.

The morning will surely come, the darkness will vanish, and thy voice pour down in golden streams breaking through the sky.

Then thy words will take wing in songs from every one of my birds' nests, and thy melodies will break forth in flowers in all my forest groves.

阳台上的一束花 [法] 亨利·马蒂斯

20

莲花盛开的那天,唉,我不自觉地走神了。我的花篮空着,却对花儿视而不见。

此刻,悲哀又一次笼罩了我。我从梦中惊醒,闻到了南风中的那一缕异香。

那淡淡的芬芳,让我的心因期待而疼痛,我觉得那是夏天急切的呼吸,寻求圆满。

那时我并不知晓,它是如此之近,它就是我的。而这份完美的芬芳,已在我内心深处开放。

On the day when the lotus bloomed, alas, my mind was straying, and I knew it not. My basket was empty and the flower remained unheeded.

Only now and again a sadness fell upon me, and I started up from my dream and felt a sweet trace of a strange fragrance in the south wind.

That vague sweetness made my heart ache with longing and it seemed to me that is was the eager breath of the summer seeking for its completion.

I knew not then that it was so near, that it was mine, and that this perfect sweetness had blossomed in the depth of my own heart.

21

我必须出航。倦怠的时光都在岸上流逝——唉，我啊！

春天把花朵开过，转身离去。如今伴随着残红，我仍在徘徊、等待。

涛声渐起，岸边的林荫道上，黄叶簌簌飘零。

你在凝望怎样的虚空！你是否感知到空中飘过的一阵悸动，还有那对岸传来的遥远歌声？

I must launch out my boat. The languid hours pass by on the shore—Alas for me!

The spring has done its flowering and taken leave. And now with the burden of faded futile flowers I wait and linger.

The waves have become clamorous, and upon the bank in the shady lane the yellow leaves flutter and fall.

What emptiness do you gaze upon! Do you not feel a thrill passing through the air with the notes of the far-away song floating from the other shore?

22

七月多雨，浓荫里，你迈着秘密的步履，如夜潜行，避开所有的守夜人。

今天，清晨合上双眼，不去理会喧闹的东风持续的呼叫，一直醒着的蓝天也蒙上了厚厚的面纱。

林野不再歌唱，家家都关闭了大门。荒凉的街上，你是孤独的行者。噢，我唯一的朋友，我最亲爱的，我家的门敞开着——不要像梦一般走过。

In the deep shadows of the rainy July, with secret steps, thou walkest, silent as night, eluding all watchers.

Today the morning has closed its eyes, heedless of the insistent calls of the loud east wind, and a thick veil has been drawn over the ever-wakeful blue sky.

The woodlands have hushed their songs, and doors are all shut at every house. Thou art the solitary wayfarer in this deserted street. Oh my only friend, my best beloved, the gates are open in my house — do not pass by like a dream.

23

暴风雨夜,你在驶向爱的旅途上吗,我的朋友?天空在失望地呻吟。

我今夜无眠。我不停地打开家门,看到外面漆黑一片,我的朋友!

我什么都看不见。我在猜想你的路在哪儿!

是从漆黑模糊的河岸,是从眉头紧蹙的树林尽头,是穿过幽暗曲折的小径,你在摸索前行来找我吗,我的朋友?

Art thou abroad on this stormy night on thy journey of love, my friend? The sky groans like one in despair.

I have no sleep tonight. Ever and again I open my door and look out on the darkness, my friend!

I can see nothing before me. I wonder where lies thy path!

By what dim shore of the ink-black river, by what far edge of the frowning forest, through what mazy depth of gloom art thou threading thy course to come to me, my friend?

房子前面的路 [法]爱德华·维亚尔

24

当一天结束,鸟儿不再歌唱,风儿也累了,就用厚厚的黑暗面纱将我蒙住,就如你用睡眠的单子裹住大地,在黄昏温柔地合上下垂的莲花瓣。

旅行尚未结束,行者的粮袋已空,衣衫褴褛,精疲力竭。请为他卸下羞耻与贫困,焕发他的新生,如同你仁慈夜色下的一朵花。

If the day is done, if birds sing no more, if the wind has flagged tired, then draw the veil of darkness thick upon me, even as thou hast wrapt the earth with the coverlet of sleep and tenderly closed the petals of the drooping lotus at dusk.

From the traveller, whose sack of provisions is empty before the voyage is ended, whose garment is torn and dust-laden, whose strength is exhausted, remove shame and poverty, and renew his life like a flower under the cover of thy kindly night.

25

在困倦的夜里，让我把自己交给睡眠，不再挣扎，把信赖托付给你。

让我不再强打精神，随便地准备对你的礼拜。

是你，将夜晚的面纱盖在白天疲惫的眼上，觉醒时满心欢喜地见到崭新的景象。

In the night of weariness let me give myself up to sleep without struggle, resting my trust upon thee.

Let me not force my flagging spirit into a poor preparation for thy worship.

It is thou who drawest the veil of night upon the tired eyes of the day to renew its sight in a fresher gladness of awakening.

26

他来了,坐在我身边,而我却没醒来。多么可恶的睡眠。哦,悲惨的我!

他在静夜里到来,手上拿着竖琴,而我的梦和琴声共鸣。

唉,为何我的夜晚如此迷失?啊,为何他的呼吸触碰了我的睡眠,而我却没见到他?

He came and sat by my side but I woke not. What a cursed sleep it was, O miserable me!

He came when the night was still; he had his harp in his hands, and my dreams became resonant with its melodies.

Alas, why are my nights all thus lost? Ah, why do I ever miss his sight whose breath touches my sleep?

27

光,光在哪儿?用欲望的烈焰将它点燃!

灯在那里,却没有一丝火苗——这是你的命运吗,我的心!唉,你还不如死去!

悲苦在敲门,她说你的主人醒着,他召唤你穿越暗夜,赶赴爱约。

天空乌云密布,阴雨连绵。我不知心绪为何如此不宁——我没明白它的含义。

瞬间的闪电,让我看见更深的阴郁。我的心摸索着那条路径,夜晚的音乐召唤我去往那里。

光,光在哪儿?用欲望的烈焰将它点燃!雷声隆隆,狂风呼啸而过。夜色如黑石一般。别让时光在暗中流逝,用你的生命点燃爱之灯。

Light, oh where is the light? Kindle it with the burning fire of desire!

There is the lamp but never a flicker of a flame, — is such thy fate, my heart! Ah, death were better by far for thee!

Misery knocks at thy door, and her message is that thy lord is wakeful, and he calls thee to the love-tryst through the darkness of night.

The sky is overcast with clouds and the rain is ceaseless. I know not what this is that stirs in me, — I know not its meaning.

A moment's flash of lightning drags down a deeper gloom on my sight, and my heart gropes for the path to where the music of the night calls me.

Light, oh where is the light? Kindle it with the burning fire of desire! It thunders and the wind rushes screaming through the void. The night is black as a black stone. Let not the hours pass by in the dark. Kindle the lamp of love with thy life.

别让时光在暗中流逝,
用你的生命点燃爱之灯。

28

约束很牢固,当我试图挣脱时,心却隐隐作痛。

我只求自由,却为自己的渴望感到羞愧。

我确认无价之宝就在你那儿,你是我最好的朋友,而我却无心清理满屋华而不实的东西。

覆盖我的,是尘埃与死亡的寿衣;我憎恨它,却又以爱意相拥。

我负债累累,错误百出,我的耻辱私密而沉重;我为自己祈福时,恐惧地颤抖,唯恐我的祈求得以实现。

Obstinate are the trammels, but my heart aches when I try to break them.

Freedom is all I want, but to hope for it I feel ashamed.

I am certain that priceless wealth is in thee, and that thou art my best friend, but I have not the heart to sweep away the tinsel that fills my room.

The shroud that covers me is a shroud of dust and death; I hate it, yet hug it in love.

My debts are large, my failures great, my shame secret and heavy; yet when I come to ask for my good, I quake in fear lest my prayer be granted.

29

以我之名被囚禁的他,在牢狱里哭泣。我一直忙碌于四处建墙,日复一日,当高墙遮住天空,在它的阴影里,迷失了真实的自我。

我以高墙为荣,用砂泥涂抹,唯恐在这名字中留有空隙;我煞费苦心,迷失了真实的自我。

He whom I enclose with my name is weeping in this dungeon. I am ever busy building this wall all around; and as this wall goes up into the sky day by day I lose sight of my true being in its dark shadow.

I take pride in this great wall, and I plaster it with dust and sand lest a least hole should be left in this name; and for all the care I take I lose sight of my true being.

30

我独自出去赴约。在寂静暗黑中尾随我的,究竟是谁?

我躲到边上让开,却无法逃脱。

他趾高气扬,地面尘土飞扬;每当我开口时,他便高声喊叫。

他就是我卑微的自己,不知羞耻;而我实在没脸和他一起,来到你的门前。

I came out alone on my way to my tryst. But who is this that follows me in the silent dark?

I move aside to avoid his presence but I escape him not.

He makes the dust rise from the earth with his swagger; he adds his loud voice to every word that I utter.

He is my own little self, my lord, he knows no shame; but I am ashamed to come to thy door in his company.

月光下的雕像 ［法］费迪南德·杜·普伊高多

31

"犯人,告诉我,是谁把你囚禁起来的?"

"是我的主人,"犯人说,"我以为在财富和权力上,我可以击败世上任何一个人。我把国王的钱财聚敛到我自己的宝库里。当倦意来袭时,我睡在了主人的床上。醒来后,我发现自己变成了囚犯,关在我自己的宝库里。"

"犯人,告诉我,是谁打造了这牢不可破的锁链?"

"是我,"犯人说,"我自己精心打造了这根锁链。我以为自己无往不胜,可以征服全世界,让我为所欲为。夜以继日,我烈焰重锤,打造出这根锁链。最终完工后,链节牢不可破,我却发现自己被锁住了。"

"Prisoner, tell me, who was it that bound you?"

"It was my master," said the prisoner, "I thought I could outdo everybody in the world in wealth and power, and I amassed in my own treasure-house the money due to my king. When sleep overcame me I lay upon the bed that was for my lord, and on waking up I found I was a prisoner in my own treasure-house."

"Prisoner, tell me, who was it that wrought this unbreakable chain?"

"It was I," said the prisoner, "who forged this chain very carefully. I thought my invincible power would hold the world captive leaving me in a freedom undisturbed. Thus night and day I worked at the chain with huge fires and cruel hard strokes. When at last the work was done and the links were complete and unbreakable, I found that it held me in its grip."

32

在这世上,那些爱我的人费尽心机,试图安稳地留住我。而你的爱不同,你的爱比他们的伟大,你让我自由。

他们从不让我独处,以免忘记他们。日子就这样一天天过去,而你还没露面。

若不是我在祷告中呼唤你,若不是我将你置于心中,你对我的爱,仍会继续等待我的爱。

By all means they try to hold me secure who love me in this world. But it is otherwise with thy love which is greater than theirs, and thou keepest me free.

Lest I forget them they never venture to leave me alone. But day passes by after day and thou art not seen.

If I call not thee in my prayers, if I keep not thee in my heart, thy love for me still waits for my love.

33

白天时,他们来到我的房子,说:"我们只用这里最小的那间。"

他们说:"我们将帮助你礼拜你的神,并卑微地只分享我们的那份恩典。"然后他们坐在角落里,安静而温顺。

到了黑夜,我发现他们强行闯入我的圣堂,贪婪地夺走了神坛上的祭品。

When it was day they came into my house and said, "We shall only take the smallest room here."

They said, "We shall help you in the worship of your God and humbly accept only our own share in his grace." And then they took their seat in a corner and they sat quiet and meek.

But in the darkness of night I find they break into my sacred shrine, strong and turbulent, and snatch with unholy greed the offerings from God's altar.

山边湖泊 [美]盖伊·罗斯

34

只要我一息尚存,我就称你为我的一切。

只要我一息尚存,我就能感知到你在我的左右,以各种方式靠近你,每时每刻,把我的爱奉献给你。

只要我一息尚存,我就永不把你隐藏。

只要我一链尚存,就与你的旨意共锁,而你的目标会在我的生命中实现——这就是你的爱之锁链。

Let only that little be left of me whereby I may name thee my all.

Let only that little be left of my will whereby I may feel thee on every side, and come to thee in everything, and offer to thee my love every moment.

Let only that little be left of me whereby I may never hide thee.

Let only that little of my fetters be left whereby I am bound with thy will, and thy purpose is carried out in my life — and that is the fetter of thy love.

35

在那里，心无所惧，头颅高昂；

在那里，知识是自由的；

在那里，世界并未因狭隘的国界分割成碎片；

在那里，言论都来自真理的深处；

在那里，不懈的努力拥抱完美；

在那里，清澈的智性之泉，不会迷失在死气沉沉的积习荒漠；

在那里，你指引心灵，思想与行动越来越开阔——

进入到自由的天堂，我的父，请让我的国家觉醒。

Where the mind is without fear and the head is held high;

Where knowledge is free;

Where the world has not been broken up into fragments by narrow domestic walls;

Where words come out from the depth of truth;

Where tireless striving stretches its arms towards perfection;

Where the clear stream of reason has not lost its way into the dreary desert sand of dead habit;

Where the mind is led forward by thee into ever-widening thought and action—

Into that heaven of freedom, my Father, let my country awake.

圣茹安的悬崖 [法]古斯塔夫·洛伊索

"看啊,黄昏已降临海岸,暮色中海鸟归巢。"

Lo, the evening has come down upon the shore and in the fading light the seabirds come flying to their nests.

第二部分 / 36—56 首

36

这是我对你的祈祷,我的主——铲去,请铲去我内心的贫穷之根。

赐予我力量,轻松地承受快乐与忧伤。

赐予我力量,让我的爱在侍奉中结出果实。

赐予我力量,永不抛弃穷人,也绝不向淫威屈膝。

赐予我力量,让我的心灵不受日常琐事的困扰。

赐予我力量,让我的力量臣服于你的爱意。

This is my prayer to thee, my lord—strike, strike at the root of penury in my heart.

Give me the strength lightly to bear my joys and sorrows.

Give me the strength to make my love fruitful in service.

Give me the strength never to disown the poor or bend my knees before insolent might.

Give me the strength to raise my mind high above daily trifles.

And give me the strength to surrender my strength to thy will with love.

佛陀 [法] 奥迪隆·雷东

37

当我筋疲力尽时,我以为我的旅程到达了终点——再也无路可走,食物已绝,只能在沉寂无名中寻找庇护。

但我发现,你的意旨知道我前路未断。当旧有的言语在舌尖消失,新的乐曲就从心底喷涌而出;旧辙方逝,新的原野便奇妙地展现出来。

I thought that my voyage had come to its end at the last limit of my power, — that the path before me was closed, that provisions were exhausted and the time come to take shelter in a silent obscurity.

But I find that thy will knows no end in me. And when old words die out on the tongue, new melodies break forth from the heart; and where the old tracks are lost, new country is revealed with its wonders.

38

我要你,只要你——让我的心不停地重复。那些让我日夜分神的所有欲望,都虚假透顶。

当夜晚隐身于黑暗,在我潜意识的深处,对光明的祈愿,仍让我呼喊——我要你,只要你。

当风暴竭尽全力捶打和平,却同时寻求和平的结局,即使我的反抗击打你的爱,所呼喊的依然是——我要你,只要你。

That I want thee, only thee — let my heart repeat without end. All desires that distract me, day and night, are false and empty to the core.

As the night keeps hidden in its gloom the petition for light, even thus in the depth of my unconsciousness rings the cry — I want thee, only thee.

As the storm still seeks its end in peace when it strikes against peace with all its might, even thus my rebellion strikes against thy love and still its cry is — I want thee, only thee.

39

当我内心焦躁不安时,请带着仁慈的甘霖降临。

当生命失去华彩时,请带着欢歌而来。

当纷乱的工作四处喧嚣,让我与世隔绝,我静默的主,请带着你的和平与安宁而来。

当我的乞讨之心被禁闭,蹲坐屋角时,我的王,以王者的威仪撞开那门。

当欲望以错觉和尘埃蒙蔽了我的心灵,哦,圣者,清醒的你,请带着电闪雷鸣而来。

When the heart is hard and parched up, come upon me with a shower of mercy.

When grace is lost from life, come with a burst of song.

When tumultuous work raises its din on all sides shutting me out from beyond, come to me, my lord of silence, with thy peace and rest.

When my beggarly heart sits crouched, shut up in a corner, break open the door, my king, and come with the ceremony of a king.

When desire blinds the mind with delusion and dust, O thou holy one, thou wakeful, come with thy light and thy thunder.

布罗多斯基的一座小房子 〔巴西〕坎迪多·波尔蒂纳里

40

很多很多天没下雨了,我的神,我的心田一片荒芜。地平线荒蛮地裸露着,没有一丝柔云笼罩,没有半点儿清霖的迹象。

如果你愿意,请把愤怒的风暴派来吧,带着黑暗的死亡气息,以闪电威震天际。

无论如何,我的主,请你召回这沉寂弥漫的酷热,它凝滞、浓郁而且残忍,用可怕的绝望燃烧心灵。

请让慈云俯下身来,如同父亲发怒时,母亲含泪的眼神。

The rain has held back for days and days, my God, in my arid heart. The horizon is fiercely naked — not the thinnest cover of a soft cloud, not the vaguest hint of a distant cool shower.

Send thy angry storm, dark with death, if it is thy wish, and with lashes of lightning startle the sky from end to end.

But call back, my lord, call back this pervading silent heat, still and keen and cruel, burning the heart with dire despair.

Let the cloud of grace bend low from above like the tearful look of the mother on the day of the father's wrath.

如果你愿意,请把愤怒的风暴派来吧,
带着黑暗的死亡气息,以闪电威震天际。

41

你躲在阴影里,在他们所有人的身后,我的爱人,你在哪里?他们推开你,在尘土飞扬的路上走过,对你视而不见。我一直守候在这儿,疲惫不堪,摆出我给你的献礼,而那些路人过来拿走我的鲜花,一枝又一枝,我的花篮几乎空了。

晨光已逝,正午亦过。在黄昏的阴影里,我睡眼蒙眬。回家的人们瞥见我,露出笑意,让我羞愧不已。我像个女乞丐般坐着,用裙子蒙住我的脸,当他们问我想要何物时,我垂眼不答。

哦,我如何才能告诉他们,我是在等候你,你也承诺会来?而我以贫穷作为自己的嫁妆,如何才能羞愧地说出口?啊,在内心深处,我以此为荣。

Where dost thou stand behind them all, my lover, hiding thyself in the shadows? They push thee and pass thee by on the dusty road, taking thee for naught. I wait here weary hours spreading my offerings for thee, while passers-by come and take my flowers, one by one, and my basket is nearly empty.

The morning time is past, and the noon. In the shade of evening my eyes are drowsy with sleep. Men going home glance at me and smile and fill me with shame. I sit like a beggar maid, drawing my skirt over my face, and when they ask me, what it is I want, I drop my eyes and answer them not.

Oh, how, indeed, could I tell them that for thee I wait, and that thou hast promised to come. How could I utter for shame that I keep for my dowry this poverty. Ah, I hug this pride in the secret of my heart.

我坐在草地上，凝望天空，梦想着你倏然来临时的华彩——灯火辉煌，车上金旗飘扬，而他们站在路边目瞪口呆，望着你下车，把我从尘土中扶起，安坐在你的身边。而我不过是个衣衫褴褛的女乞丐，羞愧却又骄傲，浑身颤抖，如同夏日微风中的一株藤蔓。

但时光流逝，却没有传来你车辇的轮声。许多游行的队伍走过，喧闹华丽。只有你静默地站在他们身后的阴影里吗？也唯我一人，哭泣着心碎无望地等你吗？

I sit on the grass and gaze upon the sky and dream of the sudden splendour of thy coming — all the lights ablaze, golden pennons flying over thy car, and they at the roadside standing agape, when they see thee come down from thy seat to raise me from the dust, and set at thy side this ragged beggar girl a-tremble with shame and pride, like a creeper in a summer breeze.

But time glides on and still no sound of the wheels of thy chariot. Many a procession passes by with noise and shouts and glamour of glory. Is it only thou who wouldst stand in the shadow silent and behind them all? And only I who would wait and weep and wear out my heart in vain longing?

有岩石的海岸线 ［巴西］坎迪多·波尔蒂纳里

42

清晨，你悄声告诉我，我们要乘舟出行，只有你和我，世上再无他人知晓，我们这次去往无境的无尽之旅。

在一望无际的海上，你含笑静听，我的歌孕育成曲，如同海浪一样自由，不受任何词语的束缚。

时辰还未到吗？还有工作要做吗？看啊，黄昏已降临海岸，暮色中海鸟归巢。

有谁知道这锁链何时会解脱，这舟儿仿佛落日最后的余晖，何时会消失在夜里？

Early in the day it was whispered that we should sail in a boat, only thou and I, and never a soul in the world would know of this our pilgrimage to no country and to no end.

In that shoreless ocean, at thy silently listening smile my songs would swell in melodies, free as waves, free from all bondage of words.

Is the time not come yet? Are there works still to do? Lo, the evening has come down upon the shore and in the fading light the seabirds come flying to their nests.

Who knows when the chains will be off, and the boat, like the last glimmer of sunset, vanish into the night?

43

那天,我没有准备好迎接你;我的国王,你竟如芸芸众生的一员,不知不觉进入我心,在我生命转眼即逝的瞬间,盖上了永恒的印鉴。

今日,我偶然照见你的印鉴,发现它们和我微不足道的日常悲喜记忆,一起混杂在尘土里,早已被我遗忘。

你并未因我在尘土中幼稚的游戏而摒弃我,我在游戏室里听到的脚步声,和回响在星际的脚步声一模一样。

The day was when I did not keep myself in readiness for thee; and entering my heart unbidden even as one of the common crowd, unknown to me, my king, thou didst press the signet of eternity upon many a fleeting moment of my life.

And today when by chance I light upon them and see thy signature, I find they have lain scattered in the dust mixed with the memory of joys and sorrows of my trivial days forgotten.

Thou didst not turn in contempt from my childish play among dust, and the steps that I heard in my playroom are the same that are echoing from star to star.

44

我满心欢喜,在路边等候,阴影追逐着光明,而初夏的雨落了下来。

从未知天际到来的信使,问候了我,又匆匆赶路;我的心里一片欢喜,微风拂过,气息香甜。

从日出到日落,我坐在门前,我知道喜悦的瞬间会突然到来,而我将亲眼见到。

这时我独自欢歌笑语,这时空气里弥漫着允诺的香气。

This is my delight, thus to wait and watch at the wayside where shadow chases light and the rain comes in the wake of the summer.

Messengers, with tidings from unknown skies, greet me and speed along the road. My heart is glad within, and the breath of the passing breeze is sweet.

From dawn till dusk I sit here before my door, and I know that of a sudden the happy moment will arrive when I shall see.

In the meanwhile I smile and I sing all alone. In the meanwhile the air is filling with the perfume of promise.

塞纳河冬天的早晨 ［法］阿尔弗雷德·西斯莱

45

你没听到他静悄悄的脚步声吗?他来了,来了,一直在向我走来。

每一个时刻,每一个年代,每日每夜,他总在走来,走来,不停地走来。

不同的心态,我唱过很多首歌,而所有的歌词都宣称:"他来了,来了,一直在向我走来。"

在芬芳明媚的四月天,穿过林间小路,他来了,来了,一直在向我走来。

在七月阴郁的雨夜,乘着乌云隆隆车辇,他来了,来了,一直在向我走来。

在漫漫悲苦中,他从我心上走来,金色的足迹,让我的喜悦闪闪发亮。

Have you not heard his silent steps? He comes, comes, ever comes.

Every moment and every age, every day and every night he comes, comes, ever comes.

Many a song have I sung in many a mood of mind, but all their notes have always proclaimed, "He comes, comes, ever comes."

In the fragrant days of sunny April through the forest path he comes, comes, ever comes.

In the rainy gloom of July nights on the thundering chariot of clouds he comes, comes, ever comes.

In sorrow after sorrow it is his steps that press upon my heart, and it is the golden touch of his feet that makes my joy to shine.

46

我不知道多久以前,你就一直在走近迎接我。日月星辰,从未将你隐藏,而让我赞颂。

从清晨到黄昏,我听见你的脚步声,你的信使进入我心,秘密地召唤我。

我只是不明白,为何今日我的生命如梦初醒,战栗的喜悦穿透我心。

似乎时辰已到,我做完工作,而你甜蜜的出现,让我闻到空气中一缕淡淡的香味儿。

I know not from what distant time thou art ever coming nearer to meet me. Thy sun and stars can never keep thee hidden from me for aye.

In many a morning and eve thy footsteps have been heard and thy messenger has come within my heart and called me in secret.

I know not only why today my life is all astir, and a feeling of tremulous joy is passing through my heart.

It is as if the time were come to wind up my work, and I feel in the air a faint smell of thy sweet presence.

47

夜色将尽,空等了他一个晚上。我担心他会在早上突然来到我的门口,而我却疲惫地睡着。噢,朋友们,把路给他留着——不要阻拦他。

如果他的脚步声没有让我醒来,那就别叫醒我。我希望不要被啁啾的鸟鸣,或是节日晨曦的狂风惊醒。就让我安睡吧,即使我的主人突然来到我的门前。

啊,我的睡眠,难得的睡眠,只等他的抚摸才会消退。啊,只有当他如梦般从漆黑睡眠中浮现,站在我面前,我闭合的双眼才会睁开,看见他的微笑之光。

让他来到我的面前,作为第一束光,第一个形体。我觉醒的灵魂初次因喜悦而战栗,缘自他的轻轻一瞥。让我自我的回归,即刻成为向他的回归。

The night is nearly spent waiting for him in vain. I fear lest in the morning he suddenly come to my door when I have fallen asleep wearied out. Oh friends, leave the way open to him — forbid him not.

If the sounds of his steps does not wake me, do not try to rouse me, I pray. I wish not to be called from my sleep by the clamorous choir of birds, by the riot of wind at the festival of morning light. Let me sleep undisturbed even if my lord comes of a sudden to my door.

Ah, my sleep, precious sleep, which only waits for his touch to vanish. Ah, my closed eyes that would open their lids only to the light of his smile when he stands before me like a dream emerging from darkness of sleep.

Let him appear before my sight as the first of all lights and all forms. The first thrill of joy to my awakened soul let it come from his glance. And let my return to myself be immediate return to him.

每一个时刻,每一个年代,每日每夜,他总在走来,走来,不停地走来。

圣瓦斯特拉胡格的海军 [法] 欧仁·布丹

48

清晨，寂静之海泛起鸟语的涟漪，路旁的花儿无比开心；云朵的缝隙洒满金辉，而我们匆匆赶路，视而不见。

我们既不欢歌，也不玩耍；我们没有去村子里做买卖，不苟言笑；在路上一点儿都没耽搁， 随着时光流逝，我们的脚步越迈越快。

日头升到中天，鸽子在阴影里咕咕叫。干枯的叶子在正午的热气里翻卷舞蹈。牧童在榕树下打着瞌睡，我在水边躺下，在草地上伸展我疲惫的四肢。

我的伙伴们嘲笑我；他们高昂着头颅，匆匆赶路；他们从不回顾，也不歇息，消失在远处的蓝雾中。他们走过很多的草地和山丘，穿越遥远的异乡。所有的荣耀都归于你，无尽之路的英雄主人！嘲弄与讥讽刺痛我，我想起身，却发现自己没有反应。我在愉悦的耻辱深处——在模糊欢喜的阴影里——让自己迷失。

The morning sea of silence broke into ripples of bird songs; and the flowers were all merry by the roadside; and the wealth of gold was scattered through the rift of the clouds while we busily went on our way and paid no heed.

We sang no glad songs nor played; we went not to the village for barter; we spoke not a word nor smiled; we lingered not on the way. We quickened our pace more and more as the time sped by.

The sun rose to the mid sky and doves cooed in the shade. Withered leaves danced and whirled in the hot air of noon. The shepherd boy drowsed and dreamed in the shadow of the banyan tree, and I laid myself down by the water and stretched my tired limbs on the grass.

My companions laughed at me in scorn; they held their heads high and hurried on; they never looked back nor rested; they vanished in the distant blue haze. They crossed many meadows and hills, and passed through strange, faraway countries. All honour to you, heroic host of the interminable path! Mockery and reproach pricked me to rise, but found no response in me. I gave myself up for lost in the depth of a glad humiliation — in the shadow of a dim delight.

阳光镶边的暗绿睡眠,缓缓地罩住我心。我忘记了自己旅行的目的,我不再挣扎,让心灵迷失在阴影和歌声之中。

当我终于醒来睁开双眼,我看见你站在我面前,用微笑淹没了我的睡眠。我曾担心路途会漫长疲惫,见到你会无比艰难!

The repose of the sun-embroidered green gloom slowly spread over my heart. I forgot for what I had travelled, and I surrendered my mind without struggle to the maze of shadows and songs.

At last, when I woke from my slumber and opened my eyes, I saw thee standing by me, flooding my sleep with thy smile. How I had feared that the path was long and wearisome, and the struggle to reach thee was hard!

海边松树 [法] 皮尔·波纳尔

49

你从王座上下来,站在我小屋的门口。

我曾在角落里独自歌唱,你听到了那歌声。你走下来,站在我的小屋门口。

你的殿堂里有很多大师,每时每刻都有人在高歌。而初学者的简单颂歌,拨动了你的爱意。一条忧伤的小溪,汇入了世界的宏伟音乐,拈着一只奖赏的花朵,你走下来,停在我小屋的门前。

You came down from your throne and stood at my cottage door.

I was singing all alone in a corner, and the melody caught your ear. You came down and stood at my cottage door.

Masters are many in your hall, and songs are sung there at all hours. But the simple carol of this novice struck at your love. One plaintive little strain mingled with the great music of the world, and with a flower for a prize you came down and stopped at my cottage door.

50

我曾沿着村里的小路挨家乞讨,那时金辇出现在远方,如梦如幻,我还猜想那是谁啊,王中之王!

我满心期待,以为我的苦日子就到头了,我站着等待主动的救助,等待散落在尘埃里的财富。

车辇停在我身边。你瞥了我一眼,微笑着下车。我感觉我命中的幸运终于来临。而你突然伸出右手说:"你有什么要给我?"

啊,你伸开手掌,向一个乞丐乞讨,这是怎样的王者玩笑!我迷惑不解,傻傻呆立,然后缓缓地从包里掏出最小的谷粒给你。

一天结束之时,我把袋子倒空在地上,大吃一惊,在一堆破烂里,发现了一粒金子。我痛哭流涕,后悔自己竟然没把一切都给你。

I had gone a-begging from door to door in the village path, when thy golden chariot appeared in the distance like a gorgeous dream and I wondered who was this King of all kings!

My hopes rose high and methought my evil days were at an end, and I stood waiting for alms to be given unasked and for wealth scattered on all sides in the dust.

The chariot stopped where I stood. Thy glance fell on me and thou camest down with a smile. I felt that the luck of my life had come at last. Then of a sudden thou didst hold out thy right hand and say "What hast thou to give to me?"

Ah, what a kingly jest was it to open thy palm to a beggar to beg! I was confused and stood undecided, and then from my wallet I slowly took out the least little grain of corn and gave it to thee.

But how great my surprise when at the day's end I emptied my bag on the floor to find a least little grain of gold among the poor heap. I bitterly wept and wished that I had had the heart to give thee my all.

51

夜色深沉。我们做完了一天的工作。我们以为最后的一个过夜的客人已经到了，村里家家户户都关上了门。只有几个人说国王会来。我们大笑着说："不会的，这怎么可能！"

好像有人在敲门，我们说那不过是风。我们熄了灯，躺下睡觉。只有某些人说："这是信使！"我们大笑着说："不可能，一定是风！"

夜深人静时，传来声响。我们睡意浓浓，想着那不过是远方的雷声。大地震颤，墙壁摇晃，扰动我们的睡眠。只有几个人说那是车轮声。我们困倦地嘟囔道："不会吧，肯定是雷声！"

夜色依然一片漆黑，鼓声响了起来。有声音传来："快醒醒！别再耽搁！"我们捂住胸口，簌簌颤抖。有人说："看啊，那是王的旗！"我们站起身来，大喊道："再没有耽搁的时间了！"

The night darkened. Our day's works had been done. We thought that the last guest had arrived for the night and the doors in the village were all shut. Only some said the king was to come. We laughed and said "No, it cannot be!"

It seemed there were knocks at the door and we said it was nothing but the wind. We put out the lamps and lay down to sleep. Only some said, "It is the messenger!" We laughed and said "No, it must be the wind!"

There came a sound in the dead of the night. We sleepily thought it was the distant thunder. The earth shook, the walls rocked, and it troubled us in our sleep. Only some said it was the sound of wheels. We said in a drowsy murmur, "No, it must be the rumbling of clouds!"

The night was still dark when the drum sounded. The voice came "Wake up! delay not!" We pressed our hands on our hearts and shuddered with fear. Some said, "Lo, there is the king's flag!" We stood up on our feet and cried "There is no time for delay!"

王来了——但灯火在哪儿，花环在哪儿？他的宝座在哪儿？噢，丢人啊！太丢人了！殿堂在哪儿？饰品在哪儿？有个人说道："哭喊无用！用空空的双手迎接他，将他带进四壁空空的屋子里吧！"

打开门，吹响海螺！夜深时刻，我们晦暗沉郁之所的王到来了。天空雷声滚滚，黑暗因闪电而战栗。拿出你破碎的席子，铺在院子里。恐怖夜晚之王，与暴风雨一起突然降临。

The king has come — but where are lights, where are wreaths? Where is the throne to seat him? Oh, shame! Oh utter shame! Where is the hall, the decorations? Someone has said, "Vain is this cry! Greet him with empty hands, lead him into thy rooms all bare!"

Open the doors, let the conch-shells be sounded! In the depth of the night has come the king of our dark, dreary house. The thunder roars in the sky. The darkness shudders with lightning. Bring out thy tattered piece of mat and spread it in the courtyard. With the storm has come of a sudden our king of the fearful night.

彼得罗波利的风景（局部） ［巴西］坎迪多·波尔蒂纳里

52

我本想向你祈求——而我没敢——你颈上的玫瑰花环。等到清晨你离开的时候,我去床上寻找碎片。如同一个乞丐,我在黎明只寻得一两片花瓣。

噢,我呀,我找的是什么?你的爱留下了何种标识?不是鲜花,不是香料,也不是香水;而是你威力无比的宝剑,火焰般闪亮,雷电般沉重。曙光照进窗口,照亮床铺。晨鸟叽叽喳喳问道:"女人,你得到了什么?"不,不是鲜花,不是香料,也不是香水——而是你可畏的宝剑。

我沉坐在那儿,惊愕不语,你这是怎样的礼物啊。我无处收藏,羞于佩带,如我般脆弱之人,抱剑在胸口会伤到我。但它是痛苦重负之誉,你的礼物,我要把它佩带于心。

I thought I should ask of thee — but I dared not — the rose wreath thou hadst on thy neck. Thus I waited for the morning, when thou didst depart, to find a few fragments on the bed. And like a beggar I searched in the dawn only for a stray petal or two.

Ah me, what is it I find? What token left of thy love? It is no flower, no spices, no vase of perfumed water. It is thy mighty sword, flashing as a flame, heavy as a bolt of thunder. The young light of morning comes through the window and spreads itself upon thy bed. The morning bird twitters and asks, "Woman, what hast thou got?" No, it is no flower, nor spices, nor vase of perfumed water — it is thy dreadful sword.

I sit and muse in wonder, what gift is this of thine. I can find no place to hide it. I am ashamed to wear it, frail as I am, and it hurts me when I press it to my bosom. Yet shall I bear in my heart this honour of the burden of pain, this gift of thine.

从此，这世上对于我不再有恐惧，在我所有的冲突中，你将无往而不胜。我带着宝剑斩断所有束缚，这世上对于我再无恐惧。

从此以后，我将抛掉所有琐碎的饰品。我心的主人，我再也不会在角落里哭泣等待，再也不会胆怯怕羞。你已将宠爱之剑赐予了我，我再也不需要玩偶的饰品！

From now there shall be no fear left for me in this world, and thou shalt be victorious in all my strife. Thou hast left death for my companion and I shall crown him with my life. Thy sword is with me to cut asunder my bonds, and there shall be no fear left for me in the world.

From now I leave off all petty decorations. Lord of my heart, no more shall there be for me waiting and weeping in corners, no more coyness and sweetness of demeanour. Thou hast given me thy sword for adornment. No more doll's decorations for me!

布罗多夫斯基的风景 [巴西]坎迪多·波尔蒂纳里

53

你的手镯真是漂亮,精工镶嵌着璀璨的星星和宝石。但在我眼里,你的宝剑更美,弧形的闪电,仿佛毗湿奴的神鸟张开双翼,完美地展示在落日愤怒的红光里。

它微微轻颤,仿佛死亡最后袭来时,生命痛苦至极的最终狂喜;如同生命纯净的火苗,被烈焰烧去俗世之感。

你的手镯真是漂亮,嵌满了闪亮的宝石;而你的宝剑,哦,雷电的主人,绝美无比,想起或看见都令人发抖。

Beautiful is thy wristlet, decked with stars and cunningly wrought in myriad-coloured jewels. But more beautiful to me thy sword with its curve of lightning like the outspread wings of the divine bird of Vishnu, perfectly poised in the angry red light of the sunset.

It quivers like the one last response of life in ecstasy of pain at the final stroke of death; it shines like the pure flame of being burning up earthly sense with one fierce flash.

Beautiful is thy wristlet, decked with starry gems; but thy sword, O lord of thunder, is wrought with uttermost beauty, terrible to behold or think of.

54

我不向你祈求任何东西;我不会在你耳边说出我的名字。当你离开时,我静默地站着。树影歪斜,我独自站在井边,女人们顶着盈满水的褐色瓦罐,都已回家,她们朝我喊道:"和我们一起走吧,快到晌午了。"而我无精打采地磨磨蹭蹭,迷失在模糊的冥想中。

我没听见你走近的脚步。当你看到我时,眼神悲哀;当你低声说话,听上去很疲惫——"啊,我是一名干渴的旅人。"我从白日梦中醒来,从我的罐里倒水在你捧着的掌上。头顶的叶子簌簌作响,布谷鸟在暗中歌唱,相思树的香气从拐弯处飘来。

当你问及我的名字,我羞愧地站立无语。真的,我什么都没为你做,你怎会记住我呢?但我心里还记得我让你喝水止渴,这让我心绪甜美。将近晌午,鸟儿疲倦地唱着歌,苦楝树的叶子在头顶沙沙作响,我坐在那儿,想了又想。

I asked nothing from thee; I uttered not my name to thine ear. When thou took'st thy leave I stood silent. I was alone by the well where the shadow of the tree fell aslant, and the women had gone home with their brown earthen pitchers full to the brim. They called me and shouted, "Come with us, the morning is wearing on to noon." But I languidly lingered awhile lost in the midst of vague musings.

I heard not thy steps as thou camest. Thine eyes were sad when they fell on me; thy voice was tired as thou spokest low — "Ah, I am a thirsty traveller." I started up from my daydreams and poured water from my jar on thy joined palms. The leaves rustled overhead; the cuckoo sang from the unseen dark, and perfume of babla flowers came from the bend of the road.

I stood speechless with shame when my name thou didst ask. Indeed, what had I done for thee to keep me in remembrance? But the memory that I could give water to thee to allay thy thirst will cling to my heart and enfold it in sweetness. The morning hour is late, the bird sings in weary notes, neem leaves rustle overhead and I sit and think and think.

海景 [巴西] 坎迪多·波尔蒂纳里

55

你心神疲倦,睡眼蒙眬。

你难道没听说,花朵在荆棘丛中正茂然开放吗?醒来吧,噢,清醒吧!别让时间白白流逝!

在石板路的尽头,在孤寂的乡野,我的朋友正独自坐着。别欺骗他。醒来吧,噢,清醒吧!

天空因正午的炎热而气喘吁吁,滚烫的沙粒铺开焦渴的斗篷——

你内心深处难道就没有了喜悦?道路之琴,就奏不出痛苦而甜美的音乐,来伴随你的每一步履?

Languor is upon your heart and the slumber is still on your eyes.

Has not the word come to you that the flower is reigning in splendour among thorns? Wake, oh awaken! Let not the time pass in vain!

At the end of the stony path, in the country of virgin solitude, my friend is sitting all alone. Deceive him not. Wake, oh awaken!

What if the sky pants and trembles with the heat of the midday sun — what if the burning sand spreads its mantle of thirst —

Is there no joy in the deep of your heart? At every footfall of yours, will not the harp of the road break out in sweet music of pain?

56

只因你的喜悦如此地盈满我,只因你俯就我。噢,万穹之主,如果你的爱不在我身上,那会在哪里?

你已接纳我,让我成为所有财富的伙伴。你的喜悦,一直在我内心上演。你的旨意,一直在我生命里实现。

为此,作为万王之王,你装扮美丽,俘获了我心。为此,你的爱,在你爱人的爱中迷失了自己,从而让人看见二者的完美结合。

Thus it is that thy joy in me is so full. Thus it is that thou hast come down to me. O thou lord of all heavens, where would be thy love if I were not?

Thou hast taken me as thy partner of all this wealth. In my heart is the endless play of thy delight. In my life thy will is ever taking shape.

And for this, thou who art the King of kings hast decked thyself in beauty to captivate my heart. And for this thy love loses itself in the love of thy lover, and there art thou seen in the perfect union of two.

花园 ［法］费迪南德·杜·普伊高多

"人们从诗句中摘取自己喜爱的诗意，而最终的意义都指向你。"

From the words of the poet men take what meanings please them; yet their last meaning points to thee.

第三部分 / 57—85 首

57

光明,我的光明,充满世界的光明,亲吻着眼睛,甜蜜着心灵!

啊,光明在舞蹈,我亲爱的,在我生命的中心;光明在拨动,我亲爱的,我爱的和弦;苍穹打开,风在狂奔,笑声传遍大地。

蝴蝶在光明之海上张开翅膀。百合和茉莉在光明的浪尖上翻滚。

光明为每一片云朵撒上金辉,我亲爱的,光明四处抛撒宝石。

树叶传递着欢歌笑语,我亲爱的,快乐无边。天堂之河漫过堤岸,喜悦的洪水四溢。

Light, my light, the world-filling light, the eye-kissing light, heart-sweetening light!

Ah, the light dances, my darling, at the centre of my life; the light strikes, my darling, the chords of my love; the sky opens, the wind runs wild, laughter passes over the earth.

The butterflies spread their sails on the sea of light. Lilies and jasmines surge up on the crest of the waves of light.

The light is shattered into gold on every cloud, my darling, and it scatters gems in profusion.

Mirth spreads from leaf to leaf, my darling, and gladness without measure. The heaven's river has drowned its banks and the flood of joy is abroad.

日诺勒的景色 [法]阿基尔·劳格

58

让欢乐的所有张力都融进我最后的歌中——这份欢乐让大地绿草如茵,让生与死这对孪生兄弟在广阔的世上舞蹈,让猛烈的风暴以笑声撼醒所有的生命。这份欢乐含泪端坐于盛开的痛苦的红莲上,倾其所有,将财富抛撒于尘埃之中,一声不响。

Let all the strains of joy mingle in my last song—the joy that makes the earth flow over in the riotous excess of the grass, the joy that sets the twin brothers, life and death, dancing over the wide world, the joy that sweeps in with the tempest, shaking and waking all life with laughter, the joy that sits still with its tears on the open red lotus of pain, and the joy that throws everything it has upon the dust, and knows not a word.

59

是的,我知道,这就是你的爱。噢,我心爱的人——在叶子上舞蹈的金光,飘过天空的闲云,吹凉我额头的清风。

晨曦涌入我的眼中——这是你传递给我心的消息。你垂下面孔,俯视着我,我的心触到了你的双脚。

Yes, I know, this is nothing but thy love, O beloved of my heart — this golden light that dances upon the leaves, these idle clouds sailing across the sky, this passing breeze leaving its coolness upon my forehead.

The morning light has flooded my eyes — this is thy message to my heart. Thy face is bent from above, thy eyes look down on my eyes, and my heart has touched thy feet.

60

在无尽世界的海滨,孩子们相会。头顶是无垠的天空,一动不动,而海水汹涌澎湃。在无尽世界的岸上,孩子们欢呼雀跃相会。

他们堆起沙堡,玩耍空贝壳。他们用枯叶编成小船,笑呵呵地推送到广阔的深海。孩子们在世界的海滨玩耍。

他们不会游泳,不懂撒网。采珠人潜海找寻珍珠,商人们乘船远航,孩子们拾起卵石又随手扔掉。他们不去寻宝,他们不知如何撒网。

海水欢快地涌上来,海滨的微笑有些苍白。负责死亡的波涛给孩子们唱着毫无意义的歌谣,就像一位晃着摇篮的母亲。大海与孩子们嬉戏,海滨的微笑有些苍白。

在无尽世界的海滨,孩子们相会。风暴在无路的天空咆哮,船只在无踪的海上沉没,死亡很遥远,孩子们在游戏。在无尽世界的海滨,孩子们盛大聚会。

On the seashore of endless worlds children meet. The infinite sky is motionless overhead and the restless water is boisterous. On the seashore of endless worlds the children meet with shouts and dances.

They build their houses with sand and they play with empty shells. With withered leaves they weave their boats and smilingly float them on the vast deep. Children have their play on the seashore of worlds.

They know not how to swim, they know not how to cast nets. Pearl fishers dive for pearls, merchants sail in their ships, while children gather pebbles and scatter them again. They seek not for hidden treasures, they know not how to cast nets.

The sea surges up with laughter and pale gleams the smile of the sea beach. Death-dealing waves sing meaningless ballads to the children, even like a mother while rocking her baby's cradle. The sea plays with children, and pale gleams the smile of the sea beach.

On the seashore of endless worlds children meet. Tempest roams in the pathless sky, ships get wrecked in the trackless water, death is abroad and children play. On the seashore of endless worlds is the great meeting of children.

海景 [巴西]坎迪多·波尔蒂纳里

61

婴儿眼里闪过的睡眠——有谁知道是从哪里来的吗?是的,传说那睡眠住在童话村里,林荫密布,萤火虫微微闪烁,吊挂着两只羞怯的魔法花蕾。睡眠就是从那里来的,亲吻着婴儿的双眼。

当婴儿睡着,颤动在嘴唇上的微笑——有谁知道它出生在哪里?是的,传说新月有一束苍白的嫩光,触碰到正在飘逝的秋云边缘,那微笑就出生在露水洗净的晨梦里——当婴儿睡着时,颤动在他嘴唇上的微笑。

当婴儿睡着,他的肢体散发出清柔的甜香——有谁知道,这甜香久藏在哪里?是的,当母亲还是少女,这甜香就在温柔静默的神秘之爱里,弥满她的心间——婴儿的肢体所散发出的清柔甜香。

The sleep that flits on baby's eyes — does anybody know from where it comes? Yes, there is a rumour that it has its dwelling where, in the fairy village among shadows of the forest dimly lit with glow-worms, there hang two timid buds of enchantment. From there it comes to kiss baby's eyes.

The smile that flickers on baby's lips when he sleeps—does anybody know where it was born? Yes, there is a rumour that a young pale beam of a crescent moon touched the edge of a vanishing autumn cloud, and there the smile was first born in the dream of a dew-washed morning — the smile that flickers on baby's lips when he sleeps.

The sweet, soft freshness that blooms on baby's limbs — does anybody know where it was hidden so long? Yes, when the mother was a young girl it lay pervading her heart in tender and silent mystery of love — the sweet, soft freshness that has bloomed on baby's limbs.

62

当我把五颜六色的玩具带给你,我的孩子,我明白为什么云朵和水面会色彩缤纷,为什么花朵会染上颜色——当我把五颜六色的玩具给你,我的孩子。

当我唱歌,让你舞蹈,我真的知道叶子里为何有音乐,为什么海浪会把齐声合唱送到大地倾听的心间——当我歌唱,让你舞蹈。

当我把糖果送到你贪婪的手上,我知道花杯里为何有蜜,果实里为何隐藏甜汁——当我把糖果送到你贪婪的手上。

当我吻你的面颊,让你微笑时,我亲爱的,我当然知道是何种快乐在晨曦中自天空倾下,以及夏日微风带给我身体的愉悦——当我吻你,让你微笑时。

When I bring to you coloured toys, my child, I understand why there is such a play of colours on clouds, on water, and why flowers are painted in tints — when I give coloured toys to you, my child.

When I sing to make you dance I truly know why there is music in leaves, and why waves send their chorus of voices to the heart of the listening earth — when I sing to make you dance.

When I bring sweet things to your greedy hands I know why there is honey in the cup of the flowers and why fruits are secretly filled with sweet juice — when I bring sweet things to your greedy hands.

When I kiss your face to make you smile, my darling, I surely understand what pleasure streams from the sky in morning light, and what delight that is which the summer breeze brings to my body — when I kiss you to make you smile.

当我把五颜六色的玩具带给你,我的孩子,

我明白为什么云朵和水面会色彩缤纷,

为什么花朵会染上颜色——

盛开的杏树 [法]阿基尔·劳格

63

你让陌生人和我成为朋友。你在他人的家里,为我留了座椅。你让远成为近,让陌生人成为兄弟。

当我必须离开熟悉的庇护所,我心惴惴不安;我忘记了,新里有旧,而你也在。

穿越新生与死亡,在此世或他生,是你引领我,也同样是你,陪伴我永生,将我心与陌生的喜悦相连。

当一个人认识了你,就再无陌生感,再无紧闭的门。噢,实现我的祷告吧,让我永远不要失去在众多游戏中触到你的狂喜。

Thou hast made me known to friends whom I knew not. Thou hast given me seats in homes not my own. Thou hast brought the distant near and made a brother of the stranger.

I am uneasy at heart when I have to leave my accustomed shelter; I forget that there abides the old in the new, and that there also thou abidest.

Through birth and death, in this world or in others, wherever thou leadest me it is thou, the same, the one companion of my endless life who ever linkest my heart with bonds of joy to the unfamiliar.

When one knows thee, then alien there is none, then no door is shut. Oh, grant me my prayer that I may never lose the bliss of the touch of the one in the play of many.

64

在荒凉河岸的斜坡上,深草丛中,我问她:"姑娘,你用斗篷遮住灯,要去向哪里?我的房子黑暗而孤寂——把你的灯借给我吧!"她抬起乌黑的眼睛,在暮色中打量了我一刻。"我来到河边,"她说,"是要在日落西山时,把我的灯漂流到河上。"我独自站在深草丛中,望着她的灯闪着微弱的火苗,无助地随波漂流。

暮色渐浓,一片静寂,我问她:"姑娘,你的灯都已点亮——你要带着灯去往哪里?我的房子黑暗而孤寂——把灯借给我吧。"她抬起乌黑的眼睛打量着我的脸,迟疑地站了一会儿,最终说道:"我是来把灯献给天空的。"我站在那儿,望着她的灯无用地燃为灰烬。

午夜无月,一片阴郁。我问她:"姑娘,你把灯抱在心口,要寻求什么呢?我的房子黑暗而孤寂——把你的灯借给我吧。"她沉吟了片刻,在暗中盯着我的脸。"我带着灯来,"她说,"是参加灯节的。"我站在那儿,望着她微弱的灯火,无用地消失在群灯之中。

On the slope of the desolate river among tall grasses I asked her, "Maiden, where do you go shading your lamp with your mantle? My house is all dark and lonesome — lend me your light!" She raised her dark eyes for a moment and looked at my face through the dusk. "I have come to the river," she said, "to float my lamp on the stream when the daylight wanes in the west." I stood alone among tall grasses and watched the timid flame of her lamp uselessly drifting in the tide.

In the silence of gathering night I asked her, "Maiden, your lights are all lit — then where do you go with your lamp? My house is all dark and lonesome — lend me your light." She raised her dark eyes on my face and stood for a moment doubtful. "I have come," she said at last, "to dedicate my lamp to the sky." I stood and watched her light uselessly burning in the void.

In the moonless gloom of midnight I ask her, "Maiden, what is your quest, holding the lamp near your heart? My house is all dark and lonesome — lend me your light." She stopped for a minute and thought and gazed at my face in the dark. "I have brought my light," she said, "to join the carnival of lamps." I stood and watched her little lamp uselessly lost among lights.

城市边缘的棚户区 〔巴西〕坎迪多·波尔蒂纳里

65

我的神,在我满溢的生命之杯里,你盛的是何种神圣的饮品?

我的诗人,你是否满心欢喜,通过我的双眼,看到你的创造;站在我的耳边,静默倾听你自己永恒的谐音?

世界在我心里编织词语,而你的喜悦为之谱曲。你满怀爱意把自己交给我,然后在我身体里感受到你自己所有的甜蜜。

What divine drink wouldst thou have, my God, from this overflowing cup of my life?

My poet, is it thy delight to see thy creation through my eyes and to stand at the portals of my ears silently to listen to thine own eternal harmony?

Thy world is weaving words in my mind and thy joy is adding music to them. Thou givest thyself to me in love and then feelest thine own entire sweetness in me.

66

她一直停留在我的生命深处,只在薄暮的微光中惊鸿一瞥;从未在晨光里打开面纱,她将是我献给你的最后的礼物,我的神,裹在我最终的歌里。

词语曾向她示爱,却未赢得她的芳心;说服曾向她伸出急切的双臂,也一无所获。

我四处漫游,把她留在我心深处,我生命的起落荣枯都围绕着她。

她统治我的思想和行动,睡眠和梦幻,却始终孤身一人。

很多男人敲我的门,约她出去,都失望地走开。

这世上,还从未有人和她见过面,她始终孤身一人,等待你的承认。

She who ever had remained in the depth of my being, in the twilight of gleams and of glimpses; she who never opened her veils in the morning light, will be my last gift to thee, my God, folded in my final song.

Words have wooed yet failed to win her; persuasion has stretched to her its eager arms in vain.

I have roamed from country to country keeping her in the core of my heart, and around her have risen and fallen the growth and decay of my life.

Over my thoughts and actions, my slumbers and dreams, she reigned yet dwelled alone and apart.

Many a man knocked at my door and asked for her and turned away in despair.

There was none in the world who ever saw her face to face, and she remained in her loneliness waiting for thy recognition.

在稻田里的稻草人 ［巴西］坎迪多·波尔蒂纳里

67

你是天空,也是鸟巢。

哦,美丽的你,巢中是你的爱,以色彩、声音、气味包裹住灵魂。

清晨来临,她右手挽着金色篮子,戴着美丽的花环,默默地为大地加冕。

然后是黄昏,越过牛羊摒弃的孤寂草场,穿过无路的小径,金色水罐里盈满和平的清风,来自西方宁静之海。

而在那里,无垠的天空舒展着,灵魂载她飞来,统治那无瑕的洁白光芒。无日,无夜,无形,无色,而且,永无言语。

Thou art the sky and thou art the nest as well.

O thou beautiful, there in the nest is thy love that encloses the soul with colours and sounds and odours.

There comes the morning with the golden basket in her right hand bearing the wreath of beauty, silently to crown the earth.

And there comes the evening over the lonely meadows deserted by herds, through trackless paths, carrying cool draughts of peace in her golden pitcher from the western ocean of rest.

But there, where spreads the infinite sky for the soul to take her flight in, reigns the stainless white radiance. There is no day nor night, nor form nor colour, and never, never a word.

68

你的阳光伸展双臂,降临我的大地,整日站在我的门前,将我的泪水、叹息和歌声的云朵,带回你的脚下。

满怀爱意,用云雾缠绕你星光熠熠的胸怀,变化莫测,并染上不停变幻的色彩。

它如此轻盈,转瞬即逝,泪眼蒙眬,幽深莫测,这就是为什么你爱它,哦,无瑕而明澈的你。这也是为什么,它能用怜悯的阴影,罩上你令人炫目的白光。

Thy sunbeam comes upon this earth of mine with arms outstretched and stands at my door the livelong day to carry back to thy feet clouds made of my tears and sighs and songs.

With fond delight thou wrappest about thy starry breast that mantle of misty cloud, turning it into numberless shapes and folds and colouring it with hues everchanging.

It is so light and so fleeting, tender and tearful and dark, that is why thou lovest it, O thou spotless and serene. And that is why it may cover thy awful white light with its pathetic shadows.

69

在我血脉中川流不息的生命之水,也流淌过世界,击节而舞。

同一生命,长成无数的草叶钻出泥土,绽放为繁花密叶。

同一生命,晃动在生与死的大海摇篮里,潮涨潮落。

生命世界的爱抚,让我的身体容光焕发。而此刻,世世代代在我血脉中舞蹈着的生命的脉搏,让我骄傲。

The same stream of life that runs through my veins night and day runs through the world and dances in rhythmic measures.

It is the same life that shoots in joy through the dust of the earth in numberless blades of grass and breaks into tumultuous waves of leaves and flowers.

It is the same life that is rocked in the ocean-cradle of birth and of death, in ebb and in flow.

I feel my limbs are made glorious by the touch of this world of life. And my pride is from the life-throb of ages dancing in my blood this moment.

海上印象 [法]尤金·布丁

70

是否能越过你,与这欢快的节奏一起开心?被抛掷,被遗弃,被拍碎在令人害怕的喜悦漩涡之中?

万物奔腾不息,从不回首,任何力量都无法拦住它们,一路奔腾。

跟上那无休止的快节奏音乐,四季舞蹈而来,又转瞬离开——颜色、曲调、香味,欢快地无尽倾泻,四处散开,又倏忽消逝。

Is it beyond thee to be glad with the gladness of this rhythm? To be tossed and lost and broken in the whirl of this fearful joy?

All things rush on, they stop not, they look not behind, no power can hold them back, they rush on.

Keeping steps with that restless, rapid music, seasons come dancing and pass away — colours, tunes, and perfumes pour in endless cascades in the abounding joy that scatters and gives up and dies every moment.

71

我要更好地利用我自己,四面打开,在你的光辉上投下彩色的影子——这才是你的幻境。

你于自身立起屏障,然后以无数的音符召唤你被阻隔的自我。而你分离的自我,已在我的体内成形。

这伤感的歌漫天回响,在多彩的眼泪和微笑中,在惊恐和希冀中;波浪起伏,梦想断续,我就是你困惑的自我。

你举起的那幅画屏,用夜与昼之笔画满了无数的图形。后面是你的座椅,用神奇的曲线编织而成,没有任何枯燥的直线。

伟大而伤感的你和我,覆盖了整个天空。你和我的歌声响起,空气生机勃勃,你和我玩着捉迷藏,时代便如此更迭。

That I should make much of myself and turn it on all sides, thus casting coloured shadows on thy radiance — such is thy *maya*.

Thou settest a barrier in thine own being and then callest thy severed self in myriad notes. This thy self-separation has taken body in me.

The poignant song is echoed through all the sky in many-coloured tears and smiles, alarms and hopes; waves rise up and sink again, dreams break and form. In me is thy own defeat of self.

This screen that thou hast raised is painted with innumerable figures with the brush of the night and the day. Behind it thy seat is woven in wondrous mysteries of curves, casting away all barren lines of straightness.

The great pageant of thee and me has overspread the sky. With the tune of thee and me all the air is vibrant, and all ages pass with the hiding and seeking of thee and me.

一个池塘 ［法］阿伯特·赖博

72

他就是最深奥的那人,用隐秘的抚摸唤醒我的生命。

他将魔法施于我的双眼,在我心弦上开心地弹奏,忽喜忽悲,抑扬顿挫。

他用金、银、青、绿倏忽即逝的色彩,编织出幻境之纱,纱褶间露出他的双脚,他的抚慰让我忘记了自我。

日月穿梭,他以种种名义,种种形态,种种狂喜与深愁,感动我心。

He it is, the innermost one, who awakens my being with his deep hidden touches.

He it is who puts his enchantment upon these eyes and joyfully plays on the chords of my heart in varied cadence of pleasure and pain.

He it is who weaves the web of this *maya* in evanescent hues of gold and silver, blue and green, and lets peep out through the folds his feet, at whose touch I forget myself.

Days come and ages pass, and it is ever he who moves my heart in many a name, in many a guise, in many a rapture of joy and of sorrow.

73

我的救赎并非来自放弃,而是在千丝万缕愉悦的联系中,我感受到自由的拥抱。

你一直在为我倾倒美酒,色香各异,将这只陶罐盈满。

我的世界将用你的火苗点燃百盏不同的灯,摆在你庙宇的祭坛前。

不,我绝不会关上我的感觉之门。所看、所听、所触的喜悦,将承受你的喜悦。

是的,我所有的幻觉将燃为喜悦的明亮,我所有的欲望将结出爱的果实。

Deliverance is not for me in renunciation. I feel the embrace of freedom in a thousand bonds of delight.

Thou ever pourest for me the fresh draught of thy wine of various colours and fragrance, filling this earthen vessel to the brim.

My world will light its hundred different lamps with thy flame and place them before the altar of thy temple.

No, I will never shut the doors of my senses. The delights of sight and hearing and touch will bear thy delight.

Yes, all my illusions will burn into illumination of joy, and all my desires ripen into fruits of love.

74

白日已尽,阴影笼罩大地。是时候了,我要去河边汲满我的水罐。

黄昏的空气中飘荡着河水悲哀的音乐,显得有些急切。啊,它呼唤我走到暮色中来。孤寂的小径阒无一人,风乍起,河面泛起阵阵涟漪。

我不知是否应该回家,还是会遇见何人。浅滩的小舟上,一个陌生人正弹拨着琵琶。

The day is no more, the shadow is upon the earth. It is time that I go to the stream to fill my pitcher.

The evening air is eager with the sad music of the water. Ah, it calls me out into the dusk. In the lonely lane there is no passer-by, the wind is up, the ripples are rampant in the river.

I know not if I shall come back home. I know not whom I shall chance to meet. There at the fording in the little boat the unknown man plays upon his lute.

75

你赐予我们尘世礼物,满足我们所有的需求,最终不灭地奔回你身边。

河流每天有功课要做,急切地流过田野和村庄;而那蜿蜒流淌的河水,最终是为了洗涤你的双脚。

鲜花芬芳了空气,而它最终的侍奉,是要把自己献给你。

对你的奉献并不会让世界贫穷。

人们从诗句中摘取自己喜爱的诗意,而最终的意义都指向你。

Thy gifts to us mortals fulfil all our needs and yet run back to thee undiminished.

The river has its everyday work to do and hastens through fields and hamlets; yet its incessant stream winds towards the washing of thy feet.

The flower sweetens the air with its perfume; yet its last service is to offer itself to thee.

Thy worship does not impoverish the world.

From the words of the poet men take what meanings please them; yet their last meaning points to thee.

76

日复一日，哦，我生命的主人，我是否可以站在你的面前？双手交叠，哦，全世界的主人，我是否可以站在你的面前？

在你孤寂沉默的广袤天空下，我是否可以满心谦卑地站在你面前？

在这纷扰忙碌、艰苦努力的世上，在匆忙的人群中，我是否可以站在你的面前？

当我完成了这世上的工作，哦，万王之王，我是否可以独自无言地站在你面前？

Day after day, O lord of my life, shall I stand before thee face to face? With folded hands, O lord of all worlds, shall I stand before thee face to face?

Under thy great sky in solitude and silence, with humble heart shall I stand before thee face to face?

In this laborious world of thine, tumultuous with toil and with struggle, among hurrying crowds shall I stand before thee face to face?

And when my work shall be done in this world, O King of kings, alone and speechless shall I stand before thee face to face?

77

我知道你是我的神,却与你分开站立——我不知你就是我自己,并未上前靠近。我知道你是我的父,在你脚下俯身——我并没有像朋友那样握住你的手。

我并未站在你降临的地方,并未将你像我自己般拥有,从而将你揽在胸前,把你当作我的同伴。

你是我兄弟中的兄弟,而我却对兄弟们视而不见,我并未和他们分享我的所得,从而将我的所有与你分享。

快乐或痛苦时,我并未和众人站在一起,这样才能与你站在一起。我畏缩着放弃生命,因此并未投身于生命的大海。

I know thee as my God and stand apart — I do not know thee as my own and come closer. I know thee as my father and bow before thy feet — I do not grasp thy hand as my friend's.

I stand not where thou comest down and ownest thyself as mine, there to clasp thee to my heart and take thee as my comrade.

Thou art the Brother amongst my brothers, but I heed them not, I divide not my earnings with them, thus sharing my all with thee.

In pleasure and in pain I stand not by the side of men, and thus stand by thee. I shrink to give up my life, and thus do not plunge into the great waters of life.

78

在创造之初,群星初次闪耀,众神在天上相聚,唱道:"哦,完美的景象!纯粹的喜悦!"

但有位神突然哭喊道——"似乎哪里的光链断了,缺了一颗星星。"

竖琴的金弦断了,歌声停了下来,众神恸哭——"失去的那颗星是最棒的,她是诸天的荣耀!"

从那天起,对她的找寻就从未停止过,众神纷纷哭喊,世界因她失去了欢乐!

只有在最沉寂的夜里,群星微笑着悄声细语——"不可能找到的!无缺的完美是在万物之上!"

When the creation was new and all the stars shone in their first splendour, the gods held their assembly in the sky and sang "Oh, the picture of perfection! The joy unalloyed!"

But one cried of a sudden — "It seems that somewhere there is a break in the chain of light and one of the stars has been lost."

The golden string of their harp snapped, their song stopped, and they cried in dismay — "Yes, that lost star was the best, she was the glory of all heavens!"

From that day the search is unceasing for her, and the cry goes on from one to the other that in her the world has lost its one joy!

Only in the deepest silence of night the stars smile and whisper among themselves — "Vain is this seeking! Unbroken perfection is over all!"

在你孤寂沉默的广袤天空下,
我是否可以满心谦卑地站在你面前?

圣瓦斯特的海湾 [法] 尤金·布丁

79

如果我今生无缘遇见你,让我随时觉知是我错过了你——让我时刻不忘,无论是梦中还是清醒时分,都让我背负这份悲恸。

当我在拥挤的集市上虚度时光,当我的手上捧满每日的盈利,让我随时觉知其实我一无所获——让我时刻不忘,无论是梦中还是清醒时分,都让我背负这份悲恸。

当我疲惫不堪喘息着坐在路边,当我在尘土中铺开床铺,让我随时觉知前路漫漫——让我时刻不忘,无论是梦中还是清醒时分,都让我背负这份悲恸。

当我的房间装饰一新,笛声悠扬,欢声笑语,让我随时觉知我尚未邀请你到我家来——让我时刻不忘,无论是梦中还是清醒时分,都让我背负这份悲恸。

If it is not my portion to meet thee in this life then let me ever feel that I have missed thy sight — let me not forget for a moment, let me carry the pangs of this sorrow in my dreams and in my wakeful hours.

As my days pass in the crowded market of this world and my hands grow full with the daily profits, let me ever feel that I have gained nothing — let me not forget for a moment, let me carry the pangs of this sorrow in my dreams and in my wakeful hours.

When I sit by the roadside, tired and panting, when I spread my bed low in the dust, let me ever feel that the long journey is still before me — let me not forget a moment, let me carry the pangs of this sorrow in my dreams and in my wakeful hours.

When my rooms have been decked out and the flutes sound and the laughter there is loud, let me ever feel that I have not invited thee to my house — let me not forget for a moment, let me carry the pangs of this sorrow in my dreams and in my wakeful hours.

80

我仿佛秋天的一朵残云,无用地在天空游荡,哦,我永远辉煌的太阳!你的触摸尚未消融我的水汽,让我成为你的一缕光线,与你分别时,我度日如年。

如若这是你的希冀,如若这是你的游戏,请将我转瞬即空的生命拿去染色镀金,让它随狂风飘去,撒落在各种奇迹之中。

再有啊,当你希望在夜里结束这场游戏,我将在黑暗中,或是洁白清晨的微笑中,在纯粹透明的清凉中,融化消失。

I am like a remnant of a cloud of autumn uselessly roaming in the sky, O my sun ever-glorious! Thy touch has not yet melted my vapour, making me one with thy light, and thus I count months and years separated from thee.

If this be thy wish and if this be thy play, then take this fleeting emptiness of mine, paint it with colours, gild it with gold, float it on the wanton wind and spread it in varied wonders.

And again when it shall be thy wish to end this play at night, I shall melt and vanish away in the dark, or it may be in a smile of the white morning, in a coolness of purity transparent.

草坪上的两只牛 [法]保罗·高更

81

在很多闲散的日子里,我哀恸逝去的时光。但时光从未逝去,我的主人。我生命的每一瞬间,都握在你的手中。

隐藏在万物的核心,你将种子滋养生芽,将蓓蕾催开,将花朵成熟为果实。

我累了,睡在闲床上,想象一切活计都已停歇。早上醒来,发现我的花园开满了奇异之花。

On many an idle day have I grieved over lost time. But it is never lost, my lord. Thou hast taken every moment of my life in thine own hands.

Hidden in the heart of things thou art nourishing seeds into sprouts, buds into blossoms, and ripening flowers into fruitfulness.

I was tired and sleeping on my idle bed and imagined all work had ceased. In the morning I woke up and found my garden full with wonders of flowers.

82

你手里有无尽的时光,我的主人。没人能计数你的时间。

日夜穿梭,时代如花朵般开开落落。你知道如何等待。

你的世纪百年相连,让一朵小小的野花臻于完美。

我们没有时间可以失去,因为没有时间,我们必须力争机会。我们太贫穷了,承担不起迟到。

因此,当我把它给予每一个急躁的、向我索要它的人,时间就流逝了,而让你的神坛最终空空如也。

日落时分,我忧心忡忡地匆匆赶来,怕你的门会关闭;我却发现尚有时间。

Time is endless in thy hands, my lord. There is none to count thy minutes.

Days and nights pass and ages bloom and fade like flowers. Thou knowest how to wait.

Thy centuries follow each other perfecting a small wild flower.

We have no time to lose, and having no time we must scramble for a chances. We are too poor to be late.

And thus it is that time goes by while I give it to every querulous man who claims it, and thine altar is empty of all offerings to the last.

At the end of the day I hasten in fear lest thy gate be shut; but I find that yet there is time.

83

母亲,我要用我悔恨的眼泪,穿成一串珍珠项链,挂在你的颈上。

群星用光镯装饰了你双脚,而我的项链要挂在你的胸上。

名利自你而来,给或不给,由你来定。而我的悔恨完全归我所有,我把它作为祭品奉献给你,你以恩慈回报于我。

Mother, I shall weave a chain of pearls for thy neck with my tears of sorrow.

The stars have wrought their anklets of light to deck thy feet, but mine will hang upon thy breast.

Wealth and fame come from thee and it is for thee to give or to withhold them. But this my sorrow is absolutely mine own, and when I bring it to thee as my offering thou rewardest me with thy grace.

84

分别的悲恸传遍世界,在无垠的天空万物成形。

分离的悲哀,整夜在星辰间静默地注视,在多雨而阴暗的七月,在簌簌作响的叶子中,成为抒情诗。

这弥漫的痛苦,在人间深化为爱欲,深化为痛苦与喜悦;在我诗人的心上,融化流淌为歌声。

It is the pang of separation that spreads throughout the world and gives birth to shapes innumerable in the infinite sky.

It is this sorrow of separation that gazes in silence all nights from star to star and becomes lyric among rustling leaves in rainy darkness of July.

It is this overspreading pain that deepens into loves and desires, into sufferings and joy in human homes; and this it is that ever melts and flows in songs through my poet's heart.

阿让特伊桥下的草地 〔法〕古斯塔夫·卡耶博特

85　当战士们初次走出主人的殿堂，他们把武力藏在了哪里？他们的盔甲和兵器在哪里？

他们走出主人的殿堂那天，看上去可怜无助，箭镞如雨般射向他们。

当战士们列队回到主人殿堂时，他们把武力藏在了哪里？

When the warriors came out first from their master's hall, where had they hid their power? Where were their armour and their arms?

They looked poor and helpless, and the arrows were showered upon them on the day they came out from their master's hall.

When the warriors marched back again to their master's hall where did they hide their power?

他们丢掉了刀剑,丢掉了弓矢;额头写着和平,当战士们列队回到主人殿堂那天,他们把生命的果实留在了身后。

They had dropped *the sword* and dropped *the bow and the arrow;*

peace was on their foreheads, and they had left the fruits of their life behind them on the day they marched back again to their master's hall.

布罗多夫斯基广场 [巴西] 坎迪多·波尔蒂纳里

"世界敬畏地肃立，低下眼看着你的双脚，所有的星辰一言不语。"

The world with eyes bent upon thy feet stands in awe with all its silent stars.

第四部分／86—103首

86

死亡,你的仆人,来到我的门口。他渡过未知之海,带着你的召唤,来到我家。

夜色晦暗,我心恐惧——但我会点灯开门,躬身迎接他。站在我门前的,是你的使者。

我会礼拜他,双手合十,双眼含泪。我会礼拜他,把我心的珍宝放在他脚下。

完成使命后,他将要回去,在我的清晨留下一团阴影;在我孤寂的家中,被遗弃的自己,将是我给你的最后的祭献。

Death, thy servant, is at my door. He has crossed the unknown sea and brought thy call to my home.

The night is dark and my heart is fearful——yet I will take up the lamp, open my gates and bow to him my welcome. It is thy messenger who stands at my door.

I will worship him with folded hands, and with tears. I will worship him placing at his feet the treasure of my heart.

He will go back with his errand done, leaving a dark shadow on my morning; and in my desolate home only my forlorn self will remain as my last offering to thee.

87

绝望,而又带着一丝希望,我在房间里四处找寻她,却没有找到。

我的房子很小,一旦丢了东西,就再也找不回来。

而你的宅邸一望无边,我的主人,为了寻找她,我不得不来到你的门前。

我站在你傍晚天空的金色华盖下,迫切地举目望你。

我已来到永恒的边缘,那里万物不灭——没有希望,没有快乐,望穿泪眼也见不到一张脸。

噢,把我虚空的生命浸入大海,将它投入最深的圆满。让我在宇宙的完满里,感受一次那失去的甜蜜触摸。

In desperate hope I go and search for her in all the corners of my room; I find her not.

My house is small and what once has gone from it can never be regained.

But infinite is thy mansion, my lord, and seeking her I have to come to thy door.

I stand under the golden canopy of thine evening sky and I lift my eager eyes to thy face.

I have come to the brink of eternity from which nothing can vanish — no hope, no happiness, no vision of a face seen through tears.

Oh, dip my emptied life into that ocean, plunge it into the deepest fullness. Let me for once feel that lost sweet touch in the allness of the universe.

88

被毁灭的庙宇之神！七弦琴的断弦不再歌颂你。傍晚的钟声不再宣告礼拜你的时辰。空气静寂，没有你的消息。

在你孤寂的居所，吹过无常的春风。它吹来鲜花的消息——无人再献花给你。

你那苍老迷路的崇拜者，一直祈求恩惠，但依然被拒绝。黄昏，当灯火和暗影湮灭于尘土，他疲惫地回到这毁坏的寺庙，满心饥饿。

被毁灭的庙宇之神，很多个节日无声地来到你的面前，很多个夜晚的礼拜黯淡流逝。

精巧艺术的大师们，营造了很多新的形象，当末日来临，那些形象便被抛入遗忘的圣河。

在不死的遗忘中，只留下了被毁灭的庙宇之神，无人礼拜。

Deity of the ruined temple! The broken strings of Vina sing no more your praise. The bells in the evening proclaim not your time of worship. The air is still and silent about you.

In your desolate dwelling comes the vagrant spring breeze. It brings the tidings of flowers — the flowers that for your worship are offered no more.

Your worshipper of old wanders ever longing for favour still refused. In the eventide, when fires and shadows mingle with the gloom of dust, he wearily comes back to the ruined temple with hunger in his heart.

Many a festival day comes to you in silence, deity of the ruined temple. Many a night of worship goes away with lamp unlit.

Many new images are built by masters of cunning art and carried to the holy stream of oblivion when their time is come.

Only the deity of the ruined temple remains unworshipped in deathless neglect.

噢,把我虚空的生命浸入大海,
将它投入最深的圆满。
让我在宇宙的完满里,
感受一次那失去的甜蜜触摸。

退潮时的海岸线 [法]尤金·布丁

89

我不再喋喋不休——这是我主的旨意。从今往后,我只悄声细语。我的心语,将用歌声低吟浅唱。

人们匆匆赶往国王的市场,所有的买家与卖家都在那里。而我却不合时宜地抛下繁忙的工作,在晌午离开。

那时,让花朵来到我的花园吧,尽管它们的时辰未到;让正午的蜜蜂慵懒地嗡嗡作响。

在正直与邪恶的争斗中,我度过了无数时光,现在,我那空虚日子的玩伴的快乐,非要把我的心拉向他;而我并不明白,为何会忽然召唤我,去面对那无关紧要的事情!

No more noisy, loud words from me — such is my master's will. Henceforth I deal in whispers. The speech of my heart will be carried on in murmurings of a song.

Men hasten to the King's market. All the buyers and sellers are there. But I have my untimely leave in the middle of the day, in the thick of work.

Let then the flowers come out in my garden, though it is not their time; and let the midday bees strike up their lazy hum.

Full many an hour have I spent in the strife of the good and the evil, but now it is the pleasure of my playmate of the empty days to draw my heart on to him; and I know not why is this sudden call to what useless inconsequence!

90

当死神去敲你门时,你会奉献什么给他?

噢,我将把我斟满的生命之杯,摆在客人面前——我绝不会让他空手而归。

当我最后的日子来临,死神敲门时,我在秋日和夏夜酿制的全部佳酿,我在繁忙生活里的一切所得,我都会摆在他的面前。

On the day when death will knock at thy door what wilt thou offer to him?

Oh, I will set before my guest the full vessel of my life — I will never let him go with empty hands.

All the sweet vintage of all my autumn days and summer nights, all the earnings and gleanings of my busy life will I place before him at the close of my days when death will knock at my door.

蓝色窗口 [法] 亨利·马蒂斯

91

噢,生命最后的圆满,死神,我的死亡,来对我低语吧!

日复一日,我一直在守望你;为了你,我承受着生命的喜悦与悲恸。

我的一切,我的所有,我的希冀和我全部的爱,一直在秘密地流向你。你最后再看我一眼,我的生命将永远成为你自己的。

新郎的花环已编好。婚礼过后,新娘将离开她的家,在寂静的夜里与她的主人独处。

O thou the last fulfilment of life, Death, my death, come and whisper to me!

Day after day I have kept watch for thee; for thee have I borne the joys and pangs of life.

All that I am, that I have, that I hope and all my love have ever flowed towards thee in depth of secrecy. One final glance from thine eyes and my life will be ever thine own.

The flowers have been woven and the garland is ready for the bridegroom. After the wedding the bride shall leave her home and meet her lord alone in the solitude of night.

92

我知道那一天终将到来,我再也看不见这片土地,生命无声离去,将最后的帘子盖在我的眼上。

然而星辰将在夜里继续守候,黎明依然会升起,时光仿佛海浪起伏,激荡着快乐与痛苦。

当我想到自己的时光终点,时光的桎梏便破碎了,死亡之光让我看见你的世界,到处散落着珠宝。最下等的座椅反而珍贵,最卑微的生命反而高贵。

那些我一直渴望而不得的,那些我得到的——都过去吧。让我真实地拥有,那些曾被我忽视摒弃的东西。

I know that the day will come when my sight of this earth shall be lost, and life will take its leave in silence, drawing the last curtain over my eyes.

Yet stars will watch at night, and morning rise as before, and hours heave like sea waves casting up pleasures and pains.

When I think of this end of my moments, the barrier of the moments breaks and I see by the light of death thy world with its careless treasures. Rare is its lowliest seat, rare is its meanest of lives.

Things that I longed for in vain and things that I got — let them pass. Let me but truly possess the things that I ever spurned and overlooked.

稻草人 [巴西] 坎迪多·波尔蒂纳里

93

我已获准离去。和我说再见吧,我的兄弟们!我向你们所有人鞠躬,转身离去。

我把家门钥匙交还——放弃了对房子的拥有。我只祈求你们最后的善语。

我们常年为邻,我得到的,多于我能够给与的。而现在天已破晓,照亮我黑暗角落的灯也已熄灭。召唤已来,我准备好启程了。

I have got my leave. Bid me farewell, my brothers! I bow to you all and take my departure.

Here I give back the keys of my door—and I give up all claims to my house. I only ask for last kind words from you.

We were neighbours for long, but I received more than I could give. Now the day has dawned and the lamp that lit my dark corner is out. A summons has come and I am ready for my journey.

94

当我告别时,祝我好运,我的朋友们!
天空晨曦初露,我的旅途美丽。

别问我会带什么过去。我启程时两手空空,只有一颗心满怀期待。

我将戴上婚礼的花环。我身上穿的不是行者红褐色的衣服,虽然路上有险阻,我心里毫无畏惧。

黄昏之星将升起,当我的旅程结束,王的门口,将奏响暮光之曲的哀歌。

At this time of my parting, wish me good luck, my friends! The sky is flushed with the dawn and my path lies beautiful.

Ask not what I have with me to take there. I start on my journey with empty hands and expectant heart.

I shall put on my wedding garland. Mine is not the red-brown dress of the traveller, and though there are dangers on the way I have no fear in mind.

The evening star will come out when my voyage is done and the plaintive notes of the twilight melodies be struck up from the King's gateway.

海景 ［巴西］坎迪多·波尔蒂纳里

95

我初次跨过此生的门槛时,自己并没有意识到。

究竟是怎样的力量,让我在这无尽的神秘中开放,仿佛一朵花蕾在午夜森林里!

清晨,当我望见光,我瞬间感到自己并不是这个世界的陌生人,一种莫名无形的神秘,以我母亲之形,将我抱在怀中。

即使如此,那同一未知的神秘将以死亡的面容出现,如我熟知的那样。因我热爱生命,我知道我也将热爱死亡。

当母亲将右乳挪开时,婴儿会哭喊,但紧接着就会在左乳找到安慰。

I was not aware of the moment when I first crossed the threshold of this life.

What was the power that made me open out into this vast mystery like a bud in the forest at midnight!

When in the morning I looked upon the light I felt in a moment that I was no stranger in this world, that the inscrutable without name and form had taken me in its arms in the form of my own mother.

Even so, in death the same unknown will appear as ever known to me. And because I love this life, I know I shall love death as well.

The child cries out when from the right breast the mother takes it away, in the very next moment to find in the left one its consolation.

96

当我离开,让这作为我告别的话语:我所见的是无法超越的。

荷花舒展在光明之海,我已品尝过隐藏的花蜜,因而受到了祝福——让这作为我告别的话语。

在这无限形体的游戏室里,我玩过了我的游戏,见到过他,而他是无形的。

我整个身体因他的触摸而颤栗,却无法触摸到他;如果死亡在此刻来临,就让它来吧——让这作为我告别的话语。

When I go from hence let this be my parting word, that what I have seen is unsurpassable.

I have tasted of the hidden honey of this lotus that expands on the ocean of light, and thus am I blessed — let this be my parting word.

In this playhouse of infinite forms I have had my play and here have I caught sight of him that is formless.

My whole body and my limbs have thrilled with his touch who is beyond touch; and if the end comes here, let it come — let this be my parting word.

月光下的卢瓦尔河边 [法] 费迪南德·杜·普伊高多

究竟是怎样的力量,
让我在这无尽的神秘中开放,
仿佛一朵花蕾在午夜森林里!

97

当我和你一起游戏时,我从未问过你是谁。我无羞无惧,我的生活热闹非凡。

清晨,你把我唤醒,就像我的伙伴一样,从一片林间空地,跑向另一片。

在那些日子里,我从未关注过你唱给我听的歌曲的含义。只是随声哼唱,而我的心随着那节奏舞蹈。

现在,当游戏的时间已过,突然降临于我的,究竟是什么?世界敬畏地肃立,低下眼看着你的双脚,所有的星辰一言不语。

When my play was with thee I never questioned who thou wert. I knew nor shyness nor fear, my life was boisterous.

In the early morning thou wouldst call me from my sleep like my own comrade and lead me running from glade to glade.

On those days I never cared to know the meaning of songs thou sangest to me. Only my voice took up the tunes, and my heart danced in their cadence.

Now, when the playtime is over, what is this sudden sight that is come upon me? The world with eyes bent upon thy feet stands in awe with all its silent stars.

98

我要以战利品,以及我失败的花环,来装饰你。我绝不会无功而逃。

我深知我的骄傲将会碰壁,我的生命将因无法承受的痛苦而炸裂,而我空虚的心将在音乐中哭泣,仿佛一根空洞的芦苇,而石头将在泪水里融化。

我深知莲花的百片花瓣不会永远闭合,隐秘的花蜜终将裸露。

一只眼睛将从蓝天凝视我,默默地召唤我。一切的一切都不会给我留下,我将在你脚下接受彻底的死亡。

I will deck thee with trophies, garlands of my defeat. It is never in my power to escape unconquered.

I surely know my pride will go to the wall, my life will burst its bonds in exceeding pain, and my empty heart will sob out in music like a hollow reed, and the stone will melt in tears.

I surely know the hundred petals of a lotus will not remain closed for ever and the secret recess of its honey will be bared.

From the blue sky an eye shall gaze upon me and summon me in silence. Nothing will be left for me, nothing whatever, and utter death shall I receive at thy feet.

海景 [巴西] 坎迪多·波尔蒂纳里

99

当我松开舵轮,我知道时辰已到,该由你掌舵了。要做的事即刻会完成。挣扎毫无用处。

那就挪开你的手,安静地承受失败,我的心,完美地静坐于被安置的地方,即是福运。

任何一阵细小的微风,都会把我的灯吹熄,而我一遍遍试图点燃它们,忘记了所有其他的事情。

但这次我会聪明起来,把席子铺在地板上,在黑暗中等候;你何时想来,我的主人,你就无声地过来坐在这里。

When I give up the helm I know that the time has come for thee to take it. What there is to do will be instantly done. Vain is this struggle.

Then take away your hands and silently put up with your defeat, my heart, and think it your good fortune to sit perfectly still where you are placed.

These my lamps are blown out at every little puff of wind, and trying to light them I forget all else again and again.

But I shall be wise this time and wait in the dark, spreading my mat on the floor; and whenever it is thy pleasure, my lord, come silently and take thy seat here.

帆船赛(局部) [巴西]玖迪多·波尔蒂纳里

100

我潜入有形海洋的深处,希望采到无形的完美珍珠。

再也不必驾着我饱经风雨的旧船,从海港驶向海港。在波涛上颠簸的日子,早已过去。

我现在只想死于不死之中。

沉入那无底的深渊,那里升起无调之弦的音乐,我将接过我生命的竖琴。

我将调试出永恒的音符,等最后的呜咽泣出,把静默的竖琴放在静默的脚下。

I dive down into the depth of the ocean of forms, hoping to gain the perfect pearl of the formless.

No more sailing from harbour to harbour with this my weather-beaten boat. The days are long passed when my sport was to be tossed on waves.

And now I am eager to die into the deathless.

Into the audience hall by the fathomless abyss where swells up the music of toneless strings I shall take this harp of my life.

I shall tune it to the notes of forever, and when it has sobbed out its last utterance, lay down my silent harp at the feet of the silent.

101

在我生命中，我一直在用歌声寻找你。歌声带着我挨家挨户寻找，让我感知到自己，寻找触摸我的世界。

我的歌声，教会了我所有的功课；把隐秘的小径展现给我，让我看见内心地平线上的群星。

歌声整日引领我，来到喜悦与痛苦的神秘国度，最终，在旅程终点的黄昏，将带我来到哪座宫殿的门口？

Ever in my life have I sought thee with my songs. It was they who led me from door to door, and with them have I felt about me, searching and touching my world.

It was my songs that taught me all the lessons I ever learnt; they showed me secret paths, they brought before my sight many a star on the horizon of my heart.

They guided me all the day long to the mysteries of the country of pleasure and pain, and, at last, to what palace gate have they brought me in the evening at the end of my journey?

102

我在人群中夸口说，我认得你。他们在我所有作品中都能见到你的画像。他们来问我："他是谁？"我不知该如何回答他们。我说："真的，我说不出来。"他们责怪我，讥讽着走开。而你微笑着坐在那儿。

我把你的传说写进不朽的歌中。秘密从我心中喷涌而出。他们来问我："告诉我你所有的含义。"我不知该如何回答他们。我说："啊，谁知道那意味着什么！"他们咧着嘴鄙夷地走开。而你微笑着坐在那儿。

I boasted among men that I had known you. They see your pictures in all works of mine. They come and ask me, "Who is he?" I know not how to answer them. I say, "Indeed, I cannot tell." They blame me and they go away in scorn. And you sit there smiling.

I put my tales of you into lasting songs. The secret gushes out from my heart. They come and ask me, "Tell me all your meanings." I know not how to answer them. I say, "Ah, who knows what they mean!" They smile and go away in utter scorn. And you sit there smiling.

103

向你致敬,我的神,

让我全部的感觉打开,触摸你脚下的世界。

仿佛七月的雨云,怀着未下之雨沉甸甸地低垂,让我全身心地躬身在你门前,

向你致敬。

In one salutation to thee, my God,

let all my senses spread out and touch this world at thy feet.

Like a rain-cloud of July hung low with its burden of unshed showers let all my mind bend down at thy door

in one salutation to thee.

让我所有歌声，将它们不同的曲调，汇合成唯一的潮水，流向静默之海，

向你致敬。

仿佛一群思乡的鹤，日夜不停，飞回它们的山巢，让我全部的生命，启程回到永恒的家园，

向你致敬。

Let all my songs gather together their diverse strains into a single current and flow to a sea of silence

in one salutation to thee.

Like a flock of homesick cranes flying night and day back to their mountain nests let all my life take its voyage to its eternal home

in one salutation to thee.

梅尼尔的森林 [法] 贝尔特·莫里索

附录

1913年诺贝尔文学奖颁奖典礼致辞

在把诺贝尔文学奖授予英印诗人拉宾德拉纳特·泰戈尔之际,学院感到非常高兴,能够把这一荣誉授予这样一位作家。他在当年写出了最优秀的具有"理想主义"倾向的诗歌,符合阿尔弗雷德·诺贝尔生前遗嘱的要求。此外,经过详尽和认真的审议,学院认为他的这些诗歌最接近规定的标准,我们没有理由犹豫,尽管诗人的名字在欧洲仍然相对不为人知,而这仅仅是由于他的家乡遥远。而且诺贝尔奖的创始人明文规定,希望在颁奖时不应顾虑候选人的国籍,我们就更没有理由不把奖项颁给泰戈尔了。

泰戈尔的《吉檀迦利:献歌》(1912年)是一部宗教诗集,他的这一部作品尤其引起了评论家们的注意。

从去年开始，这本书真正而完全地属于英语文学了。作者是以印度语接受教育和写作的，现在他给诗歌披上了一件新的外衣，在形式上同样完美，个人灵感方面也具有原创性。这使得英国、美国，乃至整个西方世界，凡是对高贵文学感兴趣的人，都能读到它们。泰戈尔完全独立于他的孟加拉诗歌知识，也不考虑宗教信仰、文学流派和党派目标的差异。他被各界誉为孟加拉诗歌艺术令人钦佩的新大师。自伊丽莎白女王时代以来，孟加拉诗歌艺术一直伴随着英国文明的扩张而不断发展。这部诗集的特色立刻赢得了热情赞赏，诗人将自己的理念与他所借鉴的内容完全融合为一个整体；他那节奏平衡的风格，引用一位英国评论家的话，是"将诗歌的女性优雅与散文的男性力量结合在一起"；他在遣词造句上被一些人称为古典主义的品位，以及他对所借用的语言表达元素的使用——简而言之，正是这些特点，使得一部作品成为具有独创性的作品；但同时，要用另一种语言将其再现，则变得更加困难。

而同样的评价，也适用于我们所读到的第二部诗集——《园丁集，爱与生命之歌》（1913年）。然而，正如作者自己所指出的那样，在这部作品中，他重新塑造而不是解释了他早期的灵感。在这里，我们看到了他的人格的另一个阶段，有感于青春爱情的体验，他时而喜悦，时而痛苦，为生活变迁感到渴望与欢乐，而其间却夹杂着对更高世界的一瞥。

泰戈尔散文故事的英文译本以《孟加拉生活的一瞥》（1913年）为题出版。虽然这些故事的形式并不带有他自己的印记，而是由另一只手呈现，但它们的内容证明了他多才多艺，观察广泛，深切同情不同类型人们的命运和经历，也证明了他在情节构建和发展方面具有的才华。

此后，泰戈尔出版了一系列诗歌，诗意地描绘了童年和家庭生活，象征性地将其题为《新月集》（1913年）；他还为美国和英国大学听众发表了许多讲演，并结集成书，名为《萨达纳：生命的实现》（1913年）。作品体现了关于人类如何获得信仰的观点，在这种信仰的光芒下，人类有可能生活下去。正是对信仰与思想之间真正关系的探索，使得泰戈尔脱颖而出，成为一位极具天赋的诗人。泰戈尔的特点是思想深邃，但更重要的是他的感情温暖，语言形象动人。的确，在富有想象力的文学领域，很少作品有如此广泛的音符和色彩，能够和谐而优雅地表达出每一种情绪，从灵魂对永恒的渴望，到天真孩童玩耍的快乐。

他的诗歌不是异域的，而是具有真正普遍的人类特性，未来我们可能会对其了解更深。然而，我们知道，诗人的动机在于努力调解两个极度分离的文明领域，这正是我们当今时代的特征标志，也构成了当今最重要的任务和问题。这项工作真正的精神，在全世界基督教宣教场所作的努力中，表现得最为清楚和纯粹。在未来，历史探究者将会知道如何更好地评价它的重要性和影响，虽然它目前隐匿在我们的视线之外，没有得到承认，或者说只得到了勉强的承认。毫无疑问，他们将在许多方面对它有更高的评价。由于这一运动，人们挖掘出鲜活的泉水，诗歌尤其可以从中获得灵感，尽管这些泉水可能与外来的溪流混合在一起，我们也许能回溯到它们真正的源头，或者会将其认定为源自梦境的深处。更特别之处在于，基督教在许多地方的布道，为方言的复兴和再生提供了首要而明确的推动力，将其从人为传统的束缚中解放出来，从而让滋养维持鲜活自然的诗歌风格的能力得以发展。

基督教作为一股复兴力量在印度也发挥了它的影响力，在那里，与宗教复兴相结合，许多方言很早就被用于文学，从而获得了稳定的地位。然而，在逐渐建立起来的新传统的压制下，它们再次僵化了。但是基督教传教的影响，远远超出了实际记录下的传教工作的范围。上个世纪，活着的方言和古代神圣的语言为控制新生文学而争斗，前者如果不是得到牺牲自我的传教士的有力扶持，此番争斗就会有截然不同的过程和结果。

1861年，拉宾德拉纳特·泰戈尔出生在孟加拉，这是英属印度最古老的省份，也是很多年前传教士先驱凯里（Carey）为推广基督教、改善当地语言而不懈努力的地方。泰戈尔出生于一个有名望的家庭，他的智慧在许多领域都有所展现。他童年和青年时成长的环境一点儿也不原始，并未束缚他对世界和生命的理解。相反，他的家庭除了对艺术有高度欣赏能力，对本民族祖先的探究精神和智慧也极为尊崇，祖先的著作被用于家中虔诚的崇拜仪式之中。在他周围也形成了一种新的文学精神，即有意识地与人们接触，了解他们的生活需要。这种新的精神在大规模的印度兵变平息之后，随着改革的坚定实施而得到了有效的发挥。

拉宾德拉纳特的父亲是一个宗教团体的主要成员，也是最热心的成员之一，他的儿子也属于这个宗教团体。这个团体被称为"梵社"，它并不是古代印度的一个教派，目的是传播对某个特定神灵的崇拜，优于对所有其他神灵的崇拜。它是在19世纪早期由一位开明而有影响力的人建立的，他对基督教的教义印象深刻，曾在英国学习过基督教教义。他努力为从过去传下来的印度本土传统提供一种与他所设想的基督教信仰的精神和含义一致的解释。从那时起，在教义上一直存在普遍的争议，这与他和他的继承者对真理的解释有关，由此细分为一些独立的教派。这个团体还有个特点，它本质上吸引的是训练有素的知识分子，从一开始就阻止其公开追随者的数量大幅增长。然而，它的间接影响，甚至对大众教育和文学的发展，都被认为是非常可观的。近年来这个团体成长起来的成员中，拉宾德拉纳特·泰戈尔的努力达到了卓越的程度。在他们看来，他是受人尊敬的大师和先知。在宗教生活和文学训练中，老师和学生之间所热切追求的那种亲密的相互作用，都得到了深刻、真挚和朴素的体现。

为了完成他一生的工作，泰戈尔学习了欧洲及印度各方面的文化，在国外旅行和在伦敦进修时，对这些文化的了解进一步扩展并成熟起来。年少时，他在自己的国家游历了很多地方，陪他的父亲一直旅行到喜马拉雅山。他在很年轻的时候就开始用孟加拉语写作，并尝试过散文、诗歌、歌词和戏剧。除了对自己国家普通人生活的描写外，他还介入了文学批评、哲学和社会学方面的问题。此前一段时间，他停下繁忙的活动，休息了一阵，因为他觉得有必要按照他的民族自古以来的惯例，在神圣的恒河的一条支流上，乘一只小船，过一段沉思的隐士生活。回到正常的生活后，他作为一个高雅智慧和自制虔诚之人，名声在自己的人民中日益鹊起。他在西孟加拉的芒果树下建立了一所露天学校，培养了许多年轻人，他们作为虔诚的门徒，在这片土地上传播他的思想。他如今已从学校退休，之前曾是英国和美国文学界的座上宾，如此度过了近一年的时光，并参加了上个夏天（1913年）在巴黎举行的宗教历史大会。

无论泰戈尔在什么地方遇到愿意接受他崇高教诲的人，人们都像接待一个带来好消息的人那样接待他，他用大家都能理解的语言，从东方宝库中带来好消息，而人们早已猜到了这宝库的存在。此外，他认为自己只是一个中介，无偿地给予他生来就能接触到的东西。他根本不急于以天才或新事物发明者的身份，在人们面前发光发热。对工作的狂热崇拜是西方世界封闭城市生活的产物，它培养了一种不安分的、有争议的精神；泰戈尔说，它为了获取利益而征服自然，"仿佛我们生活在一个充满敌意的世界里，在这个世界里，我们必须从一个不情愿的、陌生的事物安排中攫取我们想要的一切"。与所有这些令人疲惫的匆忙和混乱相反，他向我们展示了一种文化，这种文化在印度广袤、和平、神圣的森林中达到了它的完美，这种文化主要寻求灵魂的宁静和平，与自然本身的生命越来越和谐。泰戈尔在这里向我们展示的是一幅诗意的而不是历史的画面，以确认他的承诺：和平也在等待着我们。凭借与预言天赋密切相关的优势，他自由地描绘出他的创造性视野面前隐约出现的场景，时间初始时的样子。

然而，与我们中间的任何一个人一样，他远离那些我们习惯听到的在市场上传播的所谓的东方哲学，远离那些关于灵魂轮回和客观因果报应的痛苦的梦，远离那些通常被认为是印度高级文明特有的泛神论，实际上那是抽象的信仰。泰戈尔本人甚至并不承认对信仰的那种描述可以从任何先贤的深刻发言中获得权威性。他仔细研读吠陀赞美诗、《奥义书》，甚至佛陀本人的论点。他以这样一种方式，发现了对他来说无可辩驳的真理。如果说他在自然中寻求神性，那么他在那里发现了一个活生生的、具有全能特征的人格，一个包罗万象的自然之主，其超自然的精神力量同样显示在一切世俗的生命中，无论大小，尤其是在命定永恒之人的灵魂中。他把赞美、祈祷和热诚的奉献，放在这位无名之神的脚下。禁欲主义，甚至道德约束，似乎与他的那种对神的崇拜格格不入，他对神的崇拜可能是一种美学上的有神论。这种虔诚的描述与他的全部诗歌是完全一致的，给予了他平静。他为那些疲惫而忧虑的灵魂宣告和平的来临，甚至是在基督教世界的范围内。

如果我们愿意这样称呼它的话，这就是神秘主义，但不是那种神秘主义，即放弃个性、寻求全神贯注于接近虚无的"一"，而是一种把灵魂的所有才华和能力训练到最高境界的神秘主义，急切地出发去迎接创造万物的永生之父。在泰戈尔时代以前的印度，这种更为激烈的神秘主义也并非完全不为人所知，只是不在古代的苦行僧和哲学家中传播，而是以巴克提（bhakti，终身信奉一神）的形式出现，这种虔诚的本质是对上帝的深爱和依赖。自中世纪以来，在某种程度上受到基督教和其他外国宗教的影响，巴克提一直在印度教的各个阶段寻求其信仰的理想，在性质上各不相同，但在概念上均为一神教。所有那些高级形式的信仰都消失了，或者已经沉落为从前认可的形式，被大量增长的各种异教所扼杀，这些异教把那些对它们的花言巧语缺乏足够抵抗力的印度人都吸引到它们的旗下。尽管泰戈尔可能从他的先辈们的管弦交响乐中借用了一两个音符，但在这个时代，他走在更坚实的大地上。这个时代把地球上的人民在和平的道路上拉得更近，在斗争的道路上拉得更近，共同承担集体责任，并付出自己的精力向海外远方的人们致以问候和美好祝愿。泰戈尔以引人深思的画面，向我们展示了所有暂时的事物是如何被永恒淹没的：

你手里有无尽的时光，我的主人。没人能计数你的时间。

日夜穿梭，时代如花朵般开开落落。你知道如何等待。

你的世纪百年相连,让一朵小小的野花臻于完美。

我们没有时间可以失去,因为没有时间,我们必须力争机会。我们太贫穷了,承担不起迟到。

因此,当我把它给予每一个急躁的、向我索要它的人,时间就流逝了,而让你的神坛最终空空如也。

日落时分,我忧心忡忡地匆匆赶来,怕你的门会关闭;我却发现尚有时间。

(《吉檀迦利》,第82首)

哈拉尔德·赫耶尔
1913年12月10日
斯德哥尔摩

---

1 哈拉尔德·赫耶尔,瑞典科学院诺贝尔委员会主席。

泰戈尔诺贝尔文学奖获奖致辞

很高兴终于能够来到你们的国家，我想借此机会表达我对你们的感谢，谢谢你们认可我的作品，把诺贝尔奖颁发给我。

我还记得那天下午，我在英国的出版商拍电报给我，说诺贝尔奖颁给了我。当时我正在圣地尼克坦学校里，你们应该知道那所学校。当时，我们正要去学校附近的森林参加聚会，路过邮电局时，有个人追上我们，手里举着那封电报。我当时没觉得电报有多重要，就随手放进口袋，心里想着到了目的地再读。但送信的人应该是知道内容，他敦促我读一下，说内容很重要。我打开电报，读完后几乎不敢相信。起初我以为很可能是电报语言不太准确，我也许理解错了，但最后我确信了。你们可以理解，学校的孩子和老师有多么开心。让我最为感动的是这些孩子爱我，而我也深深地挚爱他们，他们所敬爱的人得了奖，他们为这荣誉感到骄傲，由此我意识到我的同胞会与我分享我所获得的荣誉。

那天下午就这样度过了。当夜色降临，我独自坐在阳台上，自问是什么原因，让西方接受了我的诗并颁奖给我——尽管我属于另一个民族，与西方的孩子们远隔千山万水。我可以向你们保证，那不是洋洋自得的感觉，而是我于心内省，感到谦卑。

我记得我的生命之作，是如何从我很年轻的时候成长起来的。差不多25岁时，在孟加拉一座鲜为人知的村庄里，我住在恒河边上的一座船屋，与世隔绝，孤独寂寞。秋天从喜马拉雅湖畔飞来的野鸭子，是我唯一活着的同伴。在那样的孤寂里，我似乎如酒水随着阳光一起流淌一样陶醉于广阔的空间，河流一直对我低语，告诉我大自然的秘密。我在孤寂中打发我的日子，梦想我的诗歌和研究，并打磨成形，通过杂志和报纸，把我的思想传递给加尔各答的公众。我不知道你们西方的诗人或作家，是否有人如此孤寂地度过年轻时的大部分时光。但我几乎可以确定，这般与世隔绝不会在西方无一席之地。

而我的生活便如此继续。在那些日子里，对于我的大多数同胞来说，我是个模糊的人物。我的意思是，在我自己的省之外，我的名字几乎无人知晓，但我非常满足于默默无名，保护自己不受大众好奇心的干扰。

后面有一段时间，我的内心感受到一种愿望，想走出那种孤寂，想为我的同胞做些事情，而不仅仅是造梦，深深冥想于生命的苦难，而要尝试着通过为我的同胞做一些具体的工作，一些具体的服务，来表达我的想法。

我所想到的一件事情、一项工作，就是教育孩子。并不是因为我特别适合做这项教育工作，我自己并未从正常的教育中获益。有段时间，我犹豫是否要承担这个任务，但我觉得我深爱大自然，自然而然地，我也深爱孩童。我开办这所学校的目的，就是想把喜悦、生命、与大自然交流的全部自由，都赋予孩子们。我小的时候曾经口吃，很多孩子去学校上学，都有过这样的经历。我曾经被教育机器碾压，粉碎了生命的喜悦与自由，而孩童对此无限渴望。我的目标，就是要给人类儿童自由和喜悦。

我招收了几个孩子在身边，教育他们，努力让他们快乐。我就是他们的玩伴，和他们做伴，分享他们的生活，觉得自己就是群里最大的孩子。我们在这种自由的氛围中一起成长。

孩子们的活力和快乐，他们的话语和歌声，让空气中充满了喜悦，我每日在那儿啜饮。黄昏日落时分，我经常一个人独坐，凝望着绿荫覆盖的街道；寂静的午后，我可以清晰地听见孩子们的声音升入空中。在我听来，那些叫嚷，那些歌声，那些快乐的声音，就如同那些树木，是从大地之心长出的；就如同生命的喷泉，升向无垠天空的胸怀。这景象把人类生命的全部呐喊带到我的心前，象征着人类喜悦与渴望的所有表达，自人性之心升起，直达天空。我看到，我明白，我们作为成年儿童，也在把我们渴望的哭喊送达无限。我在心之心内感受到它。

在这样的氛围和环境里，我写出了《吉檀迦利》中的那些诗，在印度午夜璀璨的星光下，我把诗唱给自己听。在清晨，在黄昏落日的余晖里，我写作这些歌曲，直到有一天，我强烈地感觉到要再一次走出来，去和大世界之心见面。

我能够看到，与快乐的孩子们待在一起，走出孤寂的生活，为我的同胞服务，只是我向一个更大的世界朝拜的序曲。我极度想走出来，来与西方的人性接触，因为我很想了解目前这个属于西方人的生机勃勃的时代。

西方具有全世界的力量，生命外溢于所有边界，把信息传达给远大的未来。我觉得在死去之前，一定要到西方来，会见神秘宝座的主人。神圣在此居住，它的庙宇也在这里。而且我认为，全能与渴望生命的圣人居于西方。

所以我走出来了。用孟加拉文写完《吉檀迦利》后，我把这些诗翻译成英文,一点儿都没想过要把它们出版,就我对英语的掌握来说,我没有足够的信心。但来到西方时,我把手稿带来了。如你们所知,当这些诗放到英国公众面前,那些之前有机会读到手稿的人肯定了这些诗。我被接受了,西方之心毫不迟疑地为我打开。

在我看来,这简直就是个奇迹,五十余年我远离各种活动,远离西方,却即刻被西方接纳为自己的诗人之一。我很惊讶,但又感觉到这也许有更深的含义。那些年我与世隔绝,与生命和西方精神隔离,这带来了一种更深的宁静平和,以及永恒的感觉,而这正是西方人所需要的情感,他们的生命过于活跃,在心之心内渴望平和,无限的平和。而我所契合之处,在于缪斯在我年轻时在恒河岸边绝对孤寂之中对我的训练。那些年的平和存于我的天性之中,因而我能把这平和取出,送给西方人,而西方人感动地接受了我的奉献。

我知道,我绝不可以把赞誉作为给予我个人的而接受。这是我心里的东方精神给予西方的。当西方的孩童在游戏中受伤,当他们饥饿难耐,便把脸转向东方平和的母亲,人类灵性的东方母亲。难道他们不期待食物从她而来,疲惫之夜的歇息不也来自她吗?他们怎会失望呢?

我很幸运,我来的那一刻,西方刚刚把脸转向东方寻求养分。因为我代表了东方，从西方朋友那里得到了奖赏。

我可以向你们承诺，你们给我的奖赏不会浪费于我自身。作为个人，我无权接受奖赏，所以我会为了他人使用这奖赏。我已把它捐给了我们东方学校的孩子和学生。它就如一粒种子，会被埋进土里，然后为了播种之人破土而出，为了他们的利益产出果实。我把从你们这里收到的这笔钱，用于建设和维持我最近成立的大学。在我看来，这所大学应该有西方的学生来读，会见他们东方的兄弟，一起工作，挖掘东方埋藏了多少个世纪的宝藏，了解东方的灵性资源，这些是全人类都需要的。

我提醒各位，印度文明在其辉煌时期，有过伟大的学院。当灯被点亮，光不可能隐于短程之内，它是用来照亮全世界的。印度曾有过光辉灿烂的文明、智慧与财富。她不可能只用于自己的孩子。印度为人类所有的民族都热情地敞开过大门，中国人、日本人、波斯人，所有不同的民族都来过，都有机会获得印度最好的东西，她把所有时代最好的都奉献出来，给予了全人类，无私地奉献出来。你们知道我们国家的传统，从不为了教育向学生收取任何学费，因为在印度，我们认为有知识的人有责任将知识传递给学生。不仅仅是学生来向老师学习，这也是老师必须完成的任务和使命，要把他所有的最好礼物，奉献给那些需要的人。这就是自我表达，把印度所存储的给出去，把她所拥有的最好的东西奉献出去，使其能够成为印度各省刚起步的大学的源泉。

我认为我们目前所承受的灾难，不是别的，正是晦暗隐居，我们错失了为人类奉献款待的机会，没有邀请世界分享我们拥有的最好的东西。一个多世纪以来，我们对自身的文明失去了信心，当我们接触到西方民族，他们的物质优势超过了东方的人性，超过了东方的文化，我们的教育体制没有为自己的文化制定规则。一个多世纪以来，我们的学生对自己过去的文明一无所知。因而我们不仅失去了与隐藏于自己民族遗产中的宝贵财富的接触，也失去了无私奉献的伟大荣誉，而是仅向他人乞讨，仅借用别人的文化，一直活得像个小学生。

但时机已来临，我们绝不能浪费如此的机会。我们必须尽力而为，把我们所拥有的拿出来，而不是从一个世纪到另一个世纪，从一片土地到另一片土地，在别人面前展示我们的贫穷。我们知道自己应该对从祖先那里继承的引以为荣，这个奉献的机会不应被错过——不仅仅是为了我们的民族，而是为了全世界。

出于这个原因，我下定决心建立一所国际大学，西方和东方的学生可以在这里相会，一起分享共同的精神食粮盛宴。

我可以自豪地说，你们赋予我的奖励，已经为我心里的这一远大目标做出了贡献，这让我再一次来到西方。我来邀请你们参加盛宴，在远东等着你们。我希望我的邀请不要被拒绝。我拜访过欧洲不同的国家，受到了热情的欢迎。那份欢迎有其自身的含义，西方需要东方，正如东方需要西方，所以时代已来临，他们应当相会。

我庆幸自己属于这个伟大的时代，庆幸自己为这个伟大的时代做了一些表述的工作，东方正与西方走到一起。他们相向而行，遇见彼此。他们都收到了邀请，彼此见面，携手共建新的文明，以及未来的伟大文化。

我确信，通过我的写作，一部分观点已传递给你们，即使通过翻译有些模糊。这些观点同时属于东方和西方，从东方出发，来到西方，并在此停歇，在此居住，受到欢迎，并为西方所接受。我非常幸运，能够在我的作品中阐释时代需求之声，我深深感谢你们所给予我的这个光荣的机会。我在瑞典所获得的认可将我和我的作品展示给西方公众，虽然我确信也会给我带来一些麻烦。它打破了我早已习惯的与世隔绝，而我一直习惯于孤独，尚未适应。当我站在西方人性的大广场上，我的心会收紧。我尚未习惯接受你们赞赏的伟大礼物，以及你们所给予我的欣赏方式。站在你们面前，我感到羞愧——现在正是如此。但我只想说感谢神，是他给了我这伟大的机会，让我成为团结东方和西方之心的乐器。我必须尽力而为。东方和西方之间的憎恶之情一定要和解，我一定要做些什么，我创办大学的目的就在于此。

我不认为印度精神会拒绝任何事情，拒绝任何民族，拒绝任何文化。印度精神一直强调团结的理想。团结的理想从不拒绝任何事情、民族和文化。它理解一切，是我们精神努力的最高目标，从而能以灵魂穿透万物，按照万物本来的样子加以理解，在整个宇宙中不摈弃任何一样事物——以同情和爱理解万物。这就是印度精神。如今，在政治动荡的时代，同是伟大印度的孩子们叫喊着要拒绝西方，我感到受伤。我觉得那是他们从西方学到的一课。这并非我们的任务，印度要团结人类所有的民族。

由于这个原因，我们的民族尚未得到团结。我们的问题是民族问题，这也是全世界的问题。在印度，我们有德拉威人、伊斯兰教徒、印度教徒，以及各类宗派和团体。因而，任何浅薄的政治结盟都无法吸引、满足我们，让我们感觉是真实的。我们必须更加深入，必须找到更深层的团结，各民族间的精神团结。我们必须更加深入到人类的精神，在所有民族间找到团结的伟大联结。为此，我们已做好准备。我们继承了祖先的不朽作品，那些伟大的作者宣扬团结和同情的宗教：他将万物作为自己看待，他将万物作为自己实现，他懂得真理。这需要再一次实现，不仅由东方的孩子，也要由西方的孩子实现。他们再次被提醒这些伟大不朽的真理。人类不是要与其他民族、其他个人争斗，而应致力于带来和解与和平，重建友谊和爱之联系。我们不是争斗的野兽。唯我独尊的生命统治着我们的生活，它带来隔绝，产生痛苦、嫉妒、仇恨，造成政治和商业竞争。所有这些幻象都将消失，只要我们深入神殿之心，走向爱，走向所有民族的团结。

为了印度的这个伟大目标，我创办了这所大学。我请求你们，当我现在有这个机会，我邀请你们来加入我们，不要仅把这所大学留给我们，而是要让你们自己的学生和有识之士来帮助我们，把它建成东方和西方共同的学院。希望他们能用生命做出贡献，希望我们共同实现它，使之成为人类世界不被分裂的代表。

我为此而来。我请求你们，以人类的团结之名，以爱之名，以神之名。请你们来吧，我邀请你们。

泰戈尔
1921 年 5 月 26 日
斯德哥尔摩

泰戈尔生平年表
Chronology of Tagore's Life

1861

1868—1876

出生

泰戈尔生于印度西孟加拉邦加尔各答。泰戈尔的文学修养来自家庭熏陶。他生性自由，厌恶刻板的学校生活，没有完成学校的正规课程。

上图：加尔各答的城市盾徽
左图：童年时期的泰戈尔

8—15岁

8岁开始写诗，15岁发表长诗《野花》。

上图：青少年时期的泰戈尔

1878

1880

17 岁

发表叙事诗《诗人的故事》。

赴英留学，最初在伦敦大学学院学习法律，后离开学校转为独立学习英国文学，研究西方音乐。

上图：伦敦大学学院
下图：青年泰戈尔

19 岁

回国，专门从事文学创作。

上图：泰戈尔在读书

1881—1885

20—24 岁

出版抒情诗集《暮歌》《晨歌》《画与歌》。

上图：泰戈尔在写作

1886—1890

25—29 岁

出版诗集《刚与柔》。发表剧本《国王与王后》《牺牲》。

右图：泰戈尔在舞台演戏

1891—1895

1901

30—34 岁

40 岁

发表游记《欧洲日记》。

发表《摩诃摩耶》等几十篇短篇小说。

为实现教育理想,在孟加拉博尔普尔附近的圣地尼克坦创办学校,后来该校发展为著名的印度国际大学。

上图:泰戈尔在自己创办的学校教书

1905

44岁

印度民族运动进入高潮时期,泰戈尔写了大量爱国主义诗篇,与运动其他领袖发生分歧后,过着远离现实斗争的退隐生活,埋头于文学创作。

上图:泰戈尔在孟加拉国的故居

1910—1913

49—52岁

发表长篇小说《戈拉》。
孟加拉文诗集《吉檀迦利》出版。
《吉檀迦利》英译本出版。
泰戈尔成为亚洲首位获诺贝尔文学奖的作家。

上图:1913年英文版《吉檀迦利》扉页

1922—1926

1941年8月7日

61—65 岁

发表剧本《摩克多塔拉》《红夹竹桃》等。

上图：老年泰戈尔

下图：左为爱因斯坦，右为泰戈尔

80 岁

泰戈尔在加尔各答祖宅里平静地离开人世。

成千上万的市民为他送葬。

上图：老年泰戈尔

漫步阿让特伊 [法]古斯塔夫·卡耶博特

译者 | 西蒙

　　诗人,译者。原名潘勇。生于北京,从事诗歌创作与翻译工作已逾三十年。代表译作泰戈尔文论集《生命的实现》,叶芝文论集《幻象——生命的阐释》等。

代表作品

诗集

《玻璃花园——超现实主义诗集》

《玻璃花园》

《鸟人》

《弹琴说爱》

《那束光》

译著

《幻象——生命的阐释》
叶芝文论集

《生命的实现》
泰戈尔文论集

《史蒂文斯诗集》
美国诗人史蒂文斯诗选

《吉檀迦利》
（作家榜经典名著）

画家小传

[法]皮尔·波纳尔
(1867—1947)

Pierre Bonnard

画家，版画家。以色彩闻名，被誉为二十世纪最伟大的色彩画家之一。他的作品较少运用传统图案结构，善于通过对空间、光线、色彩、构图等绘画元素的探究，对绘画对象做主观处理。作品色彩丰富，具有诗意的视觉效果，达到一种随心所欲的艺术境界。

[法]欧仁·布丹
(1824—1898)

Eugène Boudin

早期印象派风景画家。出生于水手之家，大海的印象烙印在布丹童年记忆中。布丹终其一生热爱法国西部海岸的景致，作品多描绘港口及大海风景。做过造纸厂的印刷工人，也在卢浮宫当过制版工。

[法]阿尔弗雷德·西斯莱
(1839—1899)

Alfred Sisley

法国印象派创始人之一。人生大部分时光在法国度过。主要创作风景画，风格受到印象派同道和法国著名风景画家柯罗的影响。他的画作在生前未被看重，离世后才获得好评。

[法]亨利·马蒂斯
(1869—1954)

画家,雕塑家,版画家。野兽派的创始人。马蒂斯早年学习法律,毕业后回家乡成为一名地方法院行政官。在一次患病期间,首次作画并发现其中的乐趣,从此立志成为艺术家。以马蒂斯为代表的野兽派主张印象主义的理论,促成了二十世纪第一次艺术运动。使用大胆的色彩和不拘的线条是马蒂斯的风格。对于绘画的热情,用他自己的话说:"我好像被召唤着,从此以后我不再主宰我的生活,而是它主宰我。"

Henri Matisse

[法]古斯塔夫·卡耶博特
(1848—1894)

印象派画家。作品主题与技法具有原创性,主题上擅长描绘现代生活,特别是巴黎奥曼斯大道中产阶级的日常生活景象,如巴黎改造时期各色人物的无聊与孤独感,也包括乡村和自己的家庭亲友。技法几近于摄影技法。

Gustave Caillebotte

[法]卡米耶·毕沙罗
(1830—1903)

印象派画家。喜好写生,擅长风景画,其不少后期作品是印象派中点彩画派的佳作,人像画也具有特殊的风格。1874年至1886年间,巴黎印象派画家举办的八次画展中只有他的作品每次均有展出。

Camille Pissarro

[法]阿伯特·赖博
(1849—1928)

印象派和后印象派画家。作品色彩丰富、清新,生前创作共约2000幅作品。

Albert Lebourg

[法]费迪南德·杜·普伊高多
(1864—1930)

后印象派画家。于意大利和突尼斯旅行时自学绘画。其第一批已知作品创作于1886年,同年前往法国蓬塔旺,结识查尔斯·拉瓦尔和高更。1890年其作品在法国国家美术学院参展。

Ferdinand Du Puigaudeau

[美]乔治·J. 斯坦格
(1866—1937)

George J. Stengel

印象派画家,创立了扬克斯设计学院。画作多以美国纽约州扬克斯和佛罗里达州纽霍普的风景为主要题材,以描绘安静的运河与河流风景而闻名。

[法]爱德华·维亚尔
(1868—1940)

Édouard Vuillard

纳比派代表画家。纳比派画家不依赖中心透视法,而是以纯粹主观与装饰性的观念创作。在巴黎美术学院时期,作品多为肖像画、室内画和装饰性壁屏,常以食物为题材。维亚尔实现了拉斯金、莫里斯等人提出的"艺术平等"口号。

[美]盖伊·罗斯
(1867—1925)

Guy Rose

美国加州早期印象派画家之一。早年于加州和巴黎学习绘画,后与妻子生活在法国吉维尼,在那里与莫奈相识,并受到其绘画风格影响。

[法] 贝尔特·莫里索
(1841—1895)

Berthe Morisot

印象派画家。法国评论家葛斯塔夫·杰夫华将她与玛丽·布哈可蒙和玛丽·卡萨特并列为"印象派三姝"。1864年其作品首次在学院派巴黎沙龙参展，之后连续六年入选。

[法] 保罗·高更
(1848—1903)

Paul Gauguin

印象派和后印象派代表画家。生前作品并未受过多关注。年轻时做过海员，后成为一名股票经纪人。1873年开始学画，并在1883年成为职业画家。1890年后，高更日益厌倦文明社会而渴望遁迹蛮荒，孤身前往太平洋上的塔希提岛。除去绘画之外，在雕塑、陶艺、版画和写作上也有一定的成就。高更与凡·高、塞尚被并称为后印象派三大巨匠。

[法] 古斯塔夫·洛伊索
(1865—1935)

Gustave Loiseau

后印象派画家，以绘画巴黎街头景色闻名。1890年前往法国蓬塔旺，结识许多同道画家，其中包括高更等人。之后确定了以自然风景为基础的后印象派画风。

[巴西]坎迪多·波尔蒂纳里

(1903—1962)

巴西最著名的画家之一,具有影响力的新写实主义实践者。生于巴西圣保罗州布罗多夫斯基附近的咖啡农园。画作多描绘巴西普通人的生活,绘画风格多样,用色丰富,画面内容直击人心。联合国大会大楼的壁画《战争与和平》是他的主要作品之一。其他作品包括1939年纽约世界博览会巴西厅的壁画、美国国会图书馆的壁画和巴西教育部大楼壁画等。

[法]阿基尔·劳格

(1861—1944)

后印象派画家。擅长绘画法国乡村风景,以清新的风景画闻名。

[法]奥迪隆·雷东

(1840—1916)

象征主义画派的领军人物。被德尼比作"画坛的乌拉梅"。雷东在美学上主张发挥想象而不依靠视觉印象。19世纪70年代末他开始创作石版画,共创作近200幅,总标题为《在梦中》。法国作家于斯曼称雷东的画是"病和狂的梦幻曲"。

作家榜®经典名著

读经典名著，认准作家榜

作家榜，创立于2006年的知名文化品牌，致力于促进全民阅读，推广全球经典，连续13年发布作家富豪榜系列榜单，引发各大媒体关注华语作家，努力打造"中国文化界奥斯卡"。

旗下图书品牌"作家榜经典名著"系列，精选经典中的经典，凭借好译本、优品质、高颜值的精品经典图书，成为全网常年热销的国民阅读品牌，在新一代读者中享有盛誉。

经典就读作家榜
京东官方旗舰店

经典就读作家榜
天猫官方旗舰店

经典就读作家榜
当当官方旗舰店

经典就读作家榜
拼多多旗舰店

| 策　划 | 作家榜 |
| 出　品 | |

出 品 人 ｜ 吴怀尧
总 编 辑 ｜ 周公度
产品经理 ｜ 王涵越
美术编辑 ｜ 蔡　婧
内文插图 ｜ ［巴西］坎迪多·波尔蒂纳里 等
封面插图 ｜ ［日］Tetsuhiro Wakabayashi
封面设计 ｜ 李梦琳
产品监制 ｜ 陈　俊
特约印制 ｜ 朱　毓

版权所有 ｜ 大星文化
官方电话 ｜ 021-60839180

经典就读作家榜
抖音扫码关注我

作家榜官方微博
经典好书免费送

百态人生
尽在故事会

图书在版编目（CIP）数据

吉檀迦利／（印）泰戈尔著；西蒙译. -- 杭州：浙江文艺出版社，2022.9
（作家榜经典名著）
ISBN 978-7-5339-6901-1

Ⅰ.①吉… Ⅱ.①泰… ②西… Ⅲ.①诗集－印度－现代 Ⅳ.①I351.25

中国版本图书馆CIP数据核字（2022）第112845号

责任编辑：陈园

作家榜®经典名著
读经典名著，认准作家榜

吉檀迦利

［印］泰戈尔 著　西蒙 译

全案策划
大星（上海）文化传媒有限公司

出版发行
浙江文艺出版社
杭州市体育场路347号　邮编 310006
浙江省新华书店集团有限公司 经销
上海盛通时代印刷有限公司 印刷

2022年9月第1版　2022年9月第1次印刷
889毫米×1194毫米　32开本　10.125印张
印数：1－10000　字数：179千字
书号：ISBN 978-7-5339-6901-1
定价：49.80元

版权所有　侵权必究
（如有印装质量问题影响阅读，请联系021-60839180调换）